Cowboy for Annabelle

MAIL-ORDER BRIDES ON THE RUN, BOOK 1

JOVIE GRACE

Copyright © 2022 by Jo Grafford, writing as Jovie Grace

All rights reserved.

No part of this book may be reproduced in any form without written permission from the author or publisher, except as permitted by U.S. copyright law.

ISBN: 978-1-63907-035-0

Acknowledgments

Thanks so much to my editor, Cathleen Weaver, and an enormous thank you to my beta readers — Mahasani, Debbie Turner, and PigChevy. I also want to give a shout out to my Cuppa Jo Readers on Facebook. Thank you for reading and loving my books!

For more about my books —>

Follow on Bookbub
https://www.bookbub.com/authors/jovie-grace

Follow on Amazon
https://www.amazon.com/author/joviegrace

Read FREE Bonus Stories
https://www.JoGrafford.com/bonuscontent

Join Cuppa Jo Readers
https://www.facebook.com/groups/CuppaJoReaders

Chapter 1: Desperate Times
ANNABELLE

May, 1867

Please don't be home!

Annabelle Lane stood at the end of the long, winding road that led to her childhood home. A crippled mail clerk, with a frosty beard that made her think of St. Nicholas, had brought her this far in his delivery wagon. The rest of the trip she would have to make on foot with her laundry basket in hand.

Maybe the master of the house won't be present. I'll simply knock on the front door and...

A series of rifle shots, fired in quick succession, made her wince. Unfortunately, it meant he was very much in residence. She'd been foolish to wish otherwise. She'd recognize those sounds anywhere. The aging tradesman by day and gambler by night always had his servants load a dozen or more rifles at a time for his target practice sessions. That way, he could pick them up — one right after the other — and shoot them without having to stop and reload.

It was one of the many privileges that such lavish wealth could afford. His scads of money had also enabled him to swoop in and snap up her family's plantation from the bank that had foreclosed on it a year earlier. The only thing his money had not been able to provide him, as yet, was an heir.

Out of three wives, the first two had perished during childbirth and the most recent one had met her untimely end at the base of a stairwell. An ugly rumor was circulating that it might have been more than an accident. So far, though, no one had stepped forward as a witness to the crime.

Another rumor was circulating that claimed the old codger was on the hunt for yet another wife to bear his long-hoped-for heir.

That woman will not be me.

It didn't matter to Annabelle that she was turning three and twenty today and heading straight for the dreaded spinster's "shelf." She'd happily remain alone until the end of her days before allying herself with such a known reprobate.

It was bad enough that Mr. Dale Allard Featherfall was practically old enough to be her grandfather. What was even worse, he had a distinct taste for liquor and cards.

Fortunately, it was nine o'clock in the morning, not too long past the breakfast hour. Annabelle hoped it meant the gentleman in question was currently in possession of a sober mind and temperament, especially since there was no way to avoid him. She would be walking right past his firing range. With any luck, he wouldn't see her, since his back would be facing the road.

Annabelle bit her lower lip and continued trudging up the hill, unable to stop wondering why Mr. Featherfall had hired her to launder a heaping basket of his shirts in the first place. He had more than enough servants to handle the task. The thought that he'd merely wanted an excuse to see her again made her shudder with revulsion. Her other theory wasn't any better — that he enjoyed rubbing her nose in the fact she was no longer the spoiled belle of Lane Manor. Far from it. Her life in the manor felt like eons ago. She was a working girl now, eking out a living one laundry basket and one mended shirt at a time.

It was unseasonably hot for the month of May. The sun poured its rays mercilessly down on the unshaded road. She could almost see the hard-packed earth beneath the wheel tracks growing drier and harder. Here and there, small fissures were showing. It was the longest Atlanta had gone without rain in her memory.

Once upon a time, she'd carried a parasol over her head while walking this same path. This morning her arms were so full of clean laundry that she hadn't bothered to bring it along. She'd settled for her widest bonnet instead, a white one with an enormous bow tied beneath her chin. It was fast growing damp with sweat.

The trees lining the road on her left were too far back for their branches to offer any relief from the sun. The right side of the road dipped down into a wide, grassy field. Only when Annabelle reached a short, leveled-off area in the middle of the hill did the firing range come into view.

Mr. Featherfall's servants were a good fifty yards away from her, hands flying to reload his rifles and return them to the pinewood stand in front of them.

Mr. Featherfall was pacing back and forth behind them. "Faster, lads!" he bellowed. "I do not have all day." He was a stocky man who enjoyed feasting every bit as much as imbibing. It was difficult to tell from this distance if his wide, puffy features were flushed from exertion or from yet another night of hard living. He walked with a limp that folks claimed was due to his gout, which made sense for a man his age. He possessed a surprisingly thick mop of chestnut hair that she doubted was real and hoped she'd never get close enough to find out.

He abruptly swiveled his head to look at her. She bit her

lower lip and continued walking, silently praying he would not approach. He did not so much as grace her with a raised hand in greeting, probably because he did not consider her station worthy of the gesture. Instead, he turned back around to pick up the first rifle.

A second volley of shots filled her ears. She kept her head down and her eyes on the road, hoping to reach the front steps of the veranda while he was still occupied. To her dismay, he worked his way through the line of rifles again in only a matter of seconds.

All too soon, he was limping up the hill in her direction. "Good morning to you, Miss Lane." A flick of his wrist sent one of the servant lads running to relieve her of her load.

"Good morning, sir." She kept her eyes downcast and her hands folded in front of her as he approached, hoping to present the appearance of a humble washerwoman. Her gown was a better cut than most women who earned their living this way. However, the cornflower blue silk was fast fading, and there was a small patch on the hem where she'd snagged it on something sharp.

"You are looking as lovely as usual." He ambled over to her and reached for her hand, bringing it to his lips. They were disgustingly cold and damp, despite the warm weather.

"Thank you, sir." *I am sticky and sweaty from the sun and exhausted from being stooped over a washtub for hours already this morning.* When he didn't immediately lower her hand, she added in her sweetest voice, "I couldn't help noticing your limp, sir. I hope your knee isn't causing you too much discomfort this morning."

"Your concern is touching." Dropping her hand, he jerked his head toward the house, wordlessly ordering her to follow him.

Despite his limp, he moved up the hill at a faster pace than she found comfortable, forcing her to trot in order to keep up.

She kept up a stream of chatter as they neared the home she'd grown up in. "When my grandfather's gout acted up, he used to soak his knees in—"

"Miss Lane," he interrupted tersely, "would you be so kind as to join me for a cup of tea?"

"Regrettably, I am unable to linger for a visit, sir, though your kindness is much appreciated." All she wanted was to receive her payment for her laundry services and be on her way.

Her chest ached as she beheld the two-story manor home rising before her with its stalwart columns and inviting veranda. She had so many memories both outside and inside those walls — her brothers' constant teasing and their endless pranks, family gatherings around the dinner table, spring picnics, summer teas, and winter balls. Then there were the many dancing, painting, pianoforte playing, and singing lessons that Mama had insisted her only daughter receive to mold her into a proper southern belle.

But that was then. Every inch of the plantation home, its gardens, and fields now belonged to Mr. Featherfall.

As he ambled up the porch steps ahead of her, the front door swung open. His butler stood there in a somber black suit with his white hair combed and slicked back by too much pomade.

Wheaton had once served as her family's butler in this same house. Though his gaze lit at the sight of her, he remained standing ramrod straight as Mr. Featherfall brushed past him.

Annabelle was unable to do the same. "Wheaton," she sighed, holding out her arms to him.

The older gentleman adopted a pained expression and gave her a slight headshake of warning.

"How about we move into the parlor, Miss Lane?" Mr.

Featherfall's voice was disapproving as his beady gaze flickered between her and her former employee.

"I would be delighted to, sir." With a smile of regret at Wheaton for not having more time to visit with him, she glided across the foyer into the parlor.

She was relieved when Mr. Featherfall did not invite her to take a seat on the familiar collection of blue velvet sofas and chairs. She preferred to remain standing and keep their conversation brief. There were too many memories for her in this room, too many ghosts from her past. It was fast becoming harder to breathe past the snarl of emotions rising in her throat.

Her host moved across the room to a writing desk against the wall, presumably to retrieve her payment. He took a seat there, and silence settled over the room. A minute ticked past. Then another.

Annabelle's patience grew thinner as her emotions grew threadier. Unable to remain silent any longer, she finally burst out, "As soon as you disburse my payment for the laundry, I'll be on my way. I've taken up enough of your time already, sir."

There was another extended pause before he glanced up at her. "Patience, Miss Lane. I am busy calculating the remaining balance of what you owe me."

Of what I owe you? She blinked in astonishment at him. "I beg your pardon, sir?" Alarm swirled through her as she sensed that something was terribly amiss.

"As well you should, ma'am. Your father left a mountain of debt behind. You and I must come to an agreement about how you may pay it off."

"I do not understand, sir." Dizziness shook her, making her wonder if she should have accepted his offer of tea, after all. She was parched from the sun. Her mouth felt like it was stuffed with cotton.

"Then let me explain. As you are aware, your mother

suffered from a number of illnesses over the years, and her medicine was expensive. When money grew tight during the war, I paid the balance owed to the apothecary."

Annabelle's eyebrows drew together as she tried to piece together what had happened. "Was my father aware you were making these payments?" she asked carefully.

"Does it matter?" Mr. Featherfall shot back irritably. He eyed her pointedly. "I have no doubt he would have repaid me upon his return home from the war."

But he didn't return. She scrambled for something to say that might lighten the growing tension in the room. "I don't suppose you could find it in your heart to forgive the debt?" She barely earned enough money to keep her portion of the rent paid for the boarding room. It was a fight every week to squeeze out enough coin to additionally keep food on the table.

"I think not, Miss Lane. Acts of charity do not pay the bills, nor do they cover the wages of my employees. Perhaps if your father had been more astute with his finances..." Again, he chose to leave his primary point unsaid.

Anger churned in Annabelle's belly. How dare the old toad sit there at the writing desk that had once belonged to her mother and lecture her on how a dead man should have been less charitable! The way he'd handled their family's finances had nothing whatsoever to do with why he was no longer among the living. It was cruel of Mr. Featherfall to suggest otherwise.

"Most unfortunately, I do not have the funds to pay any debts at this time," she informed him coolly. Dread pooled in her belly at the realization he had no intention of paying her for the laundry services rendered. What was worse, she had a long walk ahead of her to return to the boarding house.

He abruptly scraped back the chair and rose to face her.

"There is another way we might settle this unfortunate matter."

"Oh?" she asked faintly. For the life of her, she couldn't think of any other solutions.

He limped her way with a hand outstretched. "Marry me, Miss Lane, and all of your family's debts will be forgiven."

"What?" She recoiled in horror. His hand with its dirty fingernails might as well have been a snake.

"Marry me, and your debts will be paid in full. You will resume your role as the mistress of this house, and everything can go back to the way it was before."

Never in her life had she been so furious. His claim was utter nonsense. Words could not undo the war and everything it had taken from her. Her impeccable upbringing was the only thing that kept her from slapping him for his insolence. "How much money do I owe you, sir?" she inquired stiffly.

He named a sum that made her choke.

"And if I cannot pay it?"

"Then you will marry me," he repeated stubbornly.

"And if I refuse such a generous offer?" She ground out the words, no longer bothering to hide her sarcasm.

"Then I will have no choice but to submit your unpaid note to the debt collectors. When word gets out about your refusal to pay, I can all but guarantee that you and your friends will not be offered another job in this town."

You're threatening my friends, too? Annabelle had to dig deep to summon the poise her mother had drummed into her head for so many years. "Very well, sir. I will consider everything you have said, and I will give you my answer soon." Her heart raced sickeningly.

"You have until sundown tomorrow," he returned in such clipped tones that she had to wonder what had happened to strip him of his humanity. She was unable to detect a single drop of compassion remaining in his shriveled up soul.

Despite his enormous estate, the number of servants he employed, and his vast collection of rifles, he was to be pitied.

"I understand. Good day, sir. I'll show myself to the door." Not waiting for him to limp in her direction, she fled the room.

Wheaton was standing vigil by the door. His expression was one of pity as he opened it for her.

Her level of humility shot to an almost unbearable level. Having a former servant feel sorry for her was a new low, indeed.

"Farewell, Miss Annabelle," he said quietly.

Wrestling with too much distress to answer him, she managed a quick flutter of her hand as she lifted her skirts and hurried down the stairs. When the fabric snagged on something, she didn't bother pausing. There was a horrible ripping sound as the previously damaged hem gave way again.

She broke into a run when she reached the hard-packed wheel ruts leading away from the manor. It felt like the eyes of a thousand servants were on her shoulders as she made her escape.

She lost track of time as she ran, only slowing to a walk after she was certain she was out of sight of her childhood home. It was Saturday morning, so the streets were full of horses and wagons. None of them stopped to offer her a ride like the mail clerk had.

By the time she reached the boarding house, she was close to collapsing. Her tongue was so parched that it was sticking to the roof of her mouth. The ratty building with its peeling paint rose before her, dragging a dry sob from her. On the other side of the wall would be a room that was too small and stifling, too hot, and utterly devoid of sustenance.

Never in her life had she felt so defeated. Once the debt collectors arrived, she would be done for.

Reaching for the doorknob, she jolted when it flew open before she could twist it.

"Land sakes, sweetie! I nearly plowed right into you!" Penelope stood there in her favorite olive green gown, staring. Like Annabelle's family, hers had once reigned as Atlanta's social elite, but it no longer mattered. None of it mattered. Not their lifelong friendship. Not the vast number of memories they shared. Nothing.

Feeling like her life was officially over, Annabelle stumbled into the room. "I am sorry I startled you."

Penelope's hand shot out to encircle her wrist. "Not so fast, dearest. I can tell something is wrong, so start talking." Despite the humble way they'd been forced to live in recent months, Penelope remained every bit as much of the lady she'd been raised to be. Her long, medieval styled gown had rows of buttons holding the split sleeves together, and her hair was twisted up in a perfect coiffure. Sandy blonde ringlets danced enticingly against her cheeks.

"That old scoundrel refused to pay me for the laundry." Annabelle wanted nothing more than to fall into her bed and die.

Her friend sniffed. "I presume you're referring to Featherbottom?" It was their nickname for the dreadful creature.

"Who else?" Annabelle muttered. No sooner did she take her second step than the room erupted into cheers.

"Surprise!" a round of female voices chorused. Her friends jumped out of their hiding places to surround her in a rainbow of silk gowns as faded as her own. "Happy Birthday, Annabelle!" In addition to the angelic-looking Penelope with her penchant for humor and sass, there was Eliza Jane with her no-nonsense reading spectacles. Plus, Magnolia and Emmaline, twin sisters who'd once dreamed of going on stage and enchanting the world with their singing. Then there was the diminutive Olivia Joy, the quietest one in their tight circle of friends. She'd much rather disappear into a book or one of her watercolor paintings than carry on a conversation.

Miracle of miracles, Mag and Em produced pitchers of cider, and Eliza Jane held up a raspberry tart from the bakery down the street.

Fighting back tears at their thoughtfulness and generosity, Annabelle stumbled forward a few more steps and collapsed on the edge of her mattress. There were three sets of bunks in the room. Hers was the bottom bed closest to the door.

The cheers ground to a halt, and the smiles of her friends wavered at the sight of her torn dress and overall distress.

"Good gracious, Annabelle!" Eliza exclaimed. "Were you chased by another dog?"

Annabelle shook her head, covering a dry cough. "I'm so thirsty," she rasped.

Magnolia hastily poured her a mug of cider and pressed it into her hands. "Drink as much as you want. Mr. Hanks down at the grocer said we could fill our pitchers as many times as we want before closing time, on account of your birthday."

As Annabelle guzzled the precious liquid, she felt less like weeping. With each swallow, her anger notched up another degree. By the time she'd downed the entire mug, there might as well have been smoke coming out of her ears.

She lowered the mug to her lap. "Mr. Featherfall is trying to force me to marry him," she announced with a shiver.

Magnolia and Emmaline gave the expected dramatic shrieks and clapped their hands over their mouths. Their response was worthy of the stage they hoped to grace someday.

"Absolutely not!" Penelope's voice was coldly emphatic. "Even if he weren't such a disgusting creature, he has entirely too many dead wives in the cemetery for my tastes."

"My thoughts, exactly. Tell us everything!" Eliza Jane demanded, rocking back on the heels of her black lace-up boots. Her dark eyes glittered with indignation.

Annabelle did, not leaving out a single detail. It soothed her damaged pride and nerves to share her woes with such sympathetic listeners. "I have no way of knowing if he's even telling the truth about the debt." She paused to refill her mug of cider.

"My guess is he's lying," Eliza Jane snapped. "What a bunch of rubbish!"

"That's not all." Annabelle's tone turned bleak. "If I refuse his suit, he intends to see to it that none of us gets offered another paying job anywhere in the city."

"He can try." Penelope snorted. "I'm not convinced he has as much sway with the townsfolk as he thinks he does."

Annabelle wasn't so sure. He was a very wealthy man and could use his wealth for dastardly leverage if he wished to. "I'd honestly rather not find out." Her mouth twisted. "The moment he threatened our livelihood, I knew what I had to do."

"And that is...?" Eliza Jane prodded when Annabelle stopped to take a sip of cider.

"I think it would be best if I left town." The thought of starting over somewhere else was utterly terrifying, but Mr. Featherfall wasn't leaving her with much choice. She could not pay him back now or ever, and she most certainly wouldn't marry him.

"Are you out of your mind?" Penelope cried amidst the moans of despair from the others. "You're the heart and soul of our sisterhood. Without you, we would've never made it this far." She threw her arms up in exasperation. "No, you may not simply take off, leaving us high and dry without your clever mind and endless ideas for how to squeeze money out of a rock."

"I think leaving might be her best option, actually." It was the first time Olivia Joy had spoken up since Annabelle's return to the boarding house.

"Whose side are you on?" Eliza Jane glared at Olivia Joy, slapping her hands down on her hips.

"Annabelle's, of course." Olivia Joy produced a folded up scrap of newspaper and held it out to her. "I know you think I am being ridiculous every time I mention contacting a mail-order bride agency, but—"

"Ridiculous, preposterous, far-fetched...take your pick," Penelope sighed, snatching the paper out of her hand. "How I wish there was a bevy of fine upstanding gentlemen on the other side of the continent anxious to wed impoverished spinsters like ourselves. However, we have no way of knowing if what this advert claims is true." She gestured vehemently at the paper. "It's a cruel world out there, one we've managed to survive by sticking together. For this reason, I am not in favor of anything that pulls us apart." She held up the tiny snippet of paper between her hands, preparing to rip it into pieces.

"Wait! Let me see it first." Annabelle held out her hand for the paper, still feeling a tad queasy after how long she'd been roasting in the sun on her walk back to their room.

"I can't believe you're even considering such nonsense." Grimacing, Penelope handed it over.

"Our situation grows more desperate by the hour, I'm afraid." Annabelle smoothed open the advert and swiftly read it.

> **The Western Moon Agency** is seeking unmarried or widowed young women with adventurous spirits and strong domestic skills to wed hard-working pioneers in a new cattle town. No background too humble.

Good gracious! It was scandalous to see a company advertising for brides like someone might advertise for livestock. At the moment, though, marrying a hardworking cowboy sounded more appealing than giving in to Mr. Featherfall's heinous demands.

It's as if my life has been reduced to choosing between the frying pan and the fire. It was a depressing thought.

Before the war, Annabelle and her friends had been the beloved belles of high society. The queens of social graces — setting new standards with their lavish wardrobes, impeccable manners, and titillating conversational skills. However, the war had ended all of that when the most eligible bachelors marched off to battle and remained gone for the duration of their courting years. All too many of them had never made it home, forcing Annabelle and her friends to spend the last twelve months or so watching the highest echelons of southern society collapse at their feet.

"Well, I am certainly single," she mused, glancing up from the advert to meet the curious gazes of her friends. "I'm not so sure about my adventurous spirit or the strength of my domestic skills."

"Bah!" Eliza Jane swiped a hand through the air. "If you possessed no sense of adventure, you'd have already swooned yourself into an early grave over everything we've suffered. Pray recall it was your idea to share a boarding house, arm ourselves with mops and brooms, and canvas the streets for work." She spread her hands. "And here we are, alive to tell the tale."

Magnolia exchanged a knowing look with her sister. "As for your domestic skills, Emmaline and I were just this morning bemoaning how distressingly adept we've gotten with a washboard. It's not the life we would have chosen, but I've no doubt we could hold our own as scullery maids these days."

"Exactly." Annabelle pointed at Magnolia. "Scullery maids. That's all we are and ever will be if we remain in Atlanta. In the past few minutes, the only adjectives we've managed to come up with to describe our existence are dismal at best. Suffering. Survival. Cruel. Scrambling through the streets like rats in search of work." She waved the advert in the air. "Assuming The Western Moon Agency is a legitimate organization, they are offering something better. To trade our desperation for marriage." Uncertainties flooded her, but she pressed on. What she was proposing was not for the faint of heart. "Yes, becoming a pioneer out west would be hard work, but we're already working hard, and for what? To keep a tiny patch of roof over our heads in a roach-infested boarding house, never knowing where our next meal will come from?"

Olivia Joy studied her in horrified fascination, as if not quite believing the advert was finally being given real consideration. "What are you suggesting, Annabelle? That we rush out en masse to sign mail-order bride contracts?"

"No. Penelope is right. We have no clear idea what we're getting into. Someone needs to go first to pave the way." *And that someone needs to be me.* It was the only way out of her current dilemma.

"Oh, Annabelle!" Penelope plopped down on the bed beside her with a gusty sigh. Throwing her arms around her and hugging her tightly, she murmured, "Your courage knows no bounds, dearest."

A nervous chuckle escaped Annabelle, her heart pounding in both anticipation and trepidation. "The only thing that rivals it, perhaps, is my current level of terror." *Lord, help me to be strong for my friends.* Becoming a mail-order bride was the best opportunity that had presented itself thus far. They were desperate for relief from the grueling lives they led.

Olivia Joy left her perch on the bed across from them. "It's true bravery. I read it in a book somewhere." She joined their huddle, her delicate figure giving a small bounce on the mattress as she threw her arms around them. "Being afraid and charging forward in spite of it."

"You will write us at the first opportunity," Eliza Jane instructed fiercely. Tears of worry prickled from behind her spectacles.

"And we will follow behind you the moment you assure us it is safe to do so," Emmaline vowed with a look at her twin for affirmation. Magnolia nodded vehemently.

"None of which changes the fact that today is your birthday," Magnolia chimed in with a wobbly smile. "How about we cut into that raspberry tart to celebrate our latest, er..." She paused and glanced around the room at her friends, searching for the right word.

"Hare-brained idea?" Eliza Jane offered dryly.

"Adventure," Annabelle corrected, swallowing hard to tamp down on the apprehension rising in her throat. "Lord willing, it'll be our best one yet, ladies."

Chapter 2: Drawing Straws
ETHAN

Ethan Vasquez rolled out of bed before the first rays of dawn crept across the sky, because that was his work schedule for the next month. The following month, he would rotate back to the night shift.

He stepped into the boots he'd left beside his bed the night before and headed for the washbasin. Unable to remember if he'd tossed yesterday's water and replaced it with fresh water the night before, he splashed it on his face, hoping it was clean. It smelled clean. He completed the rest of his morning routine in silence, strapping on his weapons and grabbing a handful of dried meat strips on his way out the door. Since it wasn't Sunday, he didn't bother shaving the dark scruff prickling his face and neck.

Such was the life of a range rider. He spent each day, from sunup to sundown, guarding the ever-growing longhorn herds at the ranch where he worked. Then he awoke and did it again. It was a good life that kept a roof over his head, food in his belly, and a growing nest egg of cash in a hidden compartment that no one would find. They didn't yet have a bank in their town, and he didn't want to ride all the way to El Gato every time he needed money to purchase something.

Not all range riders were paid as much as he was. The Ford brothers had offered him a little extra to leave his last position in the mountains of New Mexico to join them in west Texas. They'd purposefully sought him out for his skill at herding cattle while keeping predators at bay — including the two-legged kind.

Ethan had first made a name for himself in the Rio Ruidoso region, where he'd outfoxed a band of rustlers by driving his herd inside a canyon. After single-handedly defending their position for nearly thirty hours from a ledge overlooking the only pass into the canyon, a federal marshal and his posse had ridden to his assistance.

No, he didn't eat horseshoes for breakfast or snack on barbed wire between meals like the legends stated. However, he was well able to oversee multiple herds at once while supervising the junior range riders. This allowed the Ford brothers to continue scavenging the countryside — often for weeks at a time — for the wild longhorns roaming the mountains and plains. They were painstakingly rounding them up and driving them home to be a part of what they hoped would soon be the biggest beef farm in Texas.

A lot of folks didn't consider the wild longhorns to be prime beef, since they tended to run on the scrawny side. However, the Fords were counting on fattening them up in time, after branding and domesticating them. Plus, they were free for the taking. A man couldn't find a better bargain than that.

Rounding up the feral cattle was part of their plan to pioneer and settle an all-new town of their own. Though they had a long way to go to get the town fully up and running, they'd already dubbed it El Vaquero, which was Spanish for cowboy.

Ethan stepped onto the front porch of his cabin. He gave his black Stetson a firm whack against his knee to knock off any remaining dust and clay clinging to it from yesterday's trail ride. Then he clapped it on his head.

A breeze whistled its way across his craggy front lawn, whipping at his plaid shirt and denim trousers. He took a moment to fill his lungs with the scent of pine trees, spring water, and good clean earth. Not that he'd ever been much of a church-goer, but living in the mountains made him feel closer to God. Sure, there were grizzly bears, mountain lions, and no shortage of rattlesnakes to share the land with, but he didn't have to endure the fuss and noise that so often came with the bigger cities. The few times he'd been forced to travel near them, or through them, always left him with the certainty that he was meant to be a mountain man.

The oldest Ford brother, Jameson, had offered Ethan a cabin on their property as a perk for serving as their lead range rider, but Ethan had insisted on purchasing twenty acres adjacent to their ranch. It was best for a man to own his home, beholden to no one. The log cabin he'd built there was a humble abode with four rooms and a loft, but it was his and it was paid for. A creek ran through his property, which would eventually irrigate the tiered gardens he intended to plant.

Someday.

When he was ready to marry again.

It wouldn't be anytime soon for a couple of reasons. He wasn't ready to put his heart through the ringer again; and other than the Fords' widowed mother, there were no women living in El Vaquero yet. It was something else her sons intended to change soon. They weren't saying how, but they'd been walking around the ranch, grinning like loons all week. He figured he was about to find out exactly how they intended to recruit ladies of marriageable age to join their pioneer venture. Knowing their reputation as pranksters, it was probably something downright laughable. Or troublesome. Something guaranteed to take up far more of Ethan's spare time than he wished.

Pushing that less than thrilling thought from his mind, he adjusted his hat brim and headed for the barn he'd built out back. It was roughly three times the size of his cabin. The Ford brothers had teased him mercilessly about building such a large shelter for one milk cow and two Mustangs, a paint named Spots and a stallion named Ranger. Ethan was content to let them laugh. The size of his barn wasn't for housing a mere three animals. It was for his future.

A future he secretly dreamed would have a family in it that he could call his own.

Ethan flung open the door of the first barn stall. "Morning, Ranger! Morning, Spots!" He swiftly fed and watered the sole longhorn, along with the reddish-brown stallion and white-spattered horse.

Spots nickered with contentment as she munched her way through her breakfast. Ranger ate just as ravenously, but he paused now and then to paw at the ground. Yesterday was his day off, so he was anxious to hit the trail. Today, Spots would be allowed to rest up until her next shift tomorrow. He'd always rotated his horses in such a manner to keep them fresh and minimize the chance for injuries.

Before saddling Ranger, he propped open the barn door, so Spots could wander outside at her leisure to graze or stretch her legs. The area was enclosed with a rustic fence he'd built himself so she wouldn't wander too far.

Ethan was soon riding across the plateau to the sprawling Ford ranch and its many outbuildings. The primary structure was an enormous three-story barn that Ethan, the Ford brothers, and the rest of their crew had constructed a little over three years ago. However, it was quickly weathering to a dark gray beneath the wind and sand storms. The farmhouse where

Jameson lived with his mother was a story-and-a-half adobe structure that they were slowly adding on to. The first addition had been a wrap-around porch. The second addition, whenever they got around to it, would be a larger dining room that could seat the entire crew for special occasions.

Paloma Ford had a lantern burning in the picture window overlooking the porch when he rode past. The homey gesture always left him with a warm feeling, making him wish he could remember the mother he'd lost at such a young age. His parents had been seasonal workers, moving from farm to farm across New Mexico in search of work. Like Paloma, his mother had been Hispanic. It was yet another thing that endeared her to him.

As Ethan neared the barn, Jameson and his next younger brother, Keegan, emerged with lanterns swinging at their sides. They were tall and rangy, with dark hair and a dark tan that bespoke their Spanish heritage. Rarely seen apart, both bore the slightly bowed legs of men who spent most of their work days in the saddle. Jameson tended to be the long-term planner, while Keegan was the doer and the shaker. The two of them always had each other's back, enjoying a closeness that Ethan often envied.

"Hold up, cowboy!" Jameson called in such a jovial voice that Ethan knew he was up to something.

He reluctantly halted Ranger. "Everything alright with the herd?"

"Bueno!" Keegan gave him a thumbs up. "There's a different matter we need to discuss," he jerked his thumb toward the house, "preferably over breakfast."

"I've already eaten."

"Gnawing on barbed wire doesn't count."

"Somebody woke up on the humorous side of the bed."

"I am always in a good humor. I was born in a good humor. Everyone knows that." Keegan swaggered closer to stroke a gloved hand down Ranger's nose and received a nip on the shoulder for his trouble. He danced back a few steps. "You and your horse, on the other hand, are perennially cranky."

"Which," Jameson held up a gloved finger, grinning eerily in the glow of the lantern, "we believe we've found the perfect solution to."

Ethan grunted. "Whatever it is, I already don't care for the sound of it."

"We knew you wouldn't." Keegan's grin widened. "That's why we're counting on some of Ma's biscuits and gravy to soften you up."

"Soften me up for what?" Ethan slid off his horse and walked alongside them the rest of the way to the farmhouse. He wouldn't give them the satisfaction of admitting it, but there probably wasn't much he wouldn't do in exchange for some of Paloma's good cooking — no matter how much of her sons' pranks he had to put up with.

"You'll find out soon enough, brother." Jameson slapped him heartily on the back, then had to dance sideways to avoid Ranger's next nip. "Biscuits and gravy first, then our big news."

Brother. Referring to Ethan as kin was another method Jameson and his five younger siblings liked to employ when they were wheedling him into doing something he didn't want to do. It was a method that rarely failed for one simple reason: The Fords truly thought of him as a brother. They teased him the same as they did each other. They included him in their family celebrations. They even saved a seat for him on Sunday mornings in their pew, which he made a point of using as little as possible. It brought back too many sad memories of his wedding and the two funerals that had followed less than a year later.

Ethan still appreciated the way they always tried to include him. They'd long since earned his trust and loyalty, and knew it. Something told him they were preparing to take advantage of that fact. Again. Fortunately, he had the promise of biscuits and gravy to sweeten the deal.

Paloma met them in the entry foyer. "My boys!" she sang out, throwing her arms wide.

Ethan pulled off his Stetson and hung it on the hall tree. Then he turned to grin at his cheery hostess. She was a sloe-eyed Hispanic woman who could almost always be found in a floral skirt and a richly embroidered white cotton blouse. This morning was no exception to that rule. Despite the number of lads she'd brought into the world, her figure remained lithe and trim, no doubt from how hard she worked every day of the week as the only pioneer woman in their town.

Jameson and Keegan enveloped her in bear hugs, taking turns lifting her off her feet and spinning her until she was dizzy.

"Enough!" She finally shooed them away, chuckling. "Any more of that and I'll topple clean over like a drunkard."

She wiggled her fingers impatiently at Ethan to bring him forward. "Come on. You're mine, too, like it or not."

"I like it," he assured, gathering her close in a tender embrace. "Mighty grateful for all you've done for me." There was no need to say more. She understood what a mess he'd been inside his head the day her sons had hired him and brought him back to the ranch.

She gave him an extra hug before taking a step back, though she didn't immediately let him go. Sliding her hands down his arms, she cocked her head at him as she continued to loosely hold his wrists. "I'm proud of you, Ethan. Proud of how you've kept on living. I know it hasn't been easy being all alone in that cabin of yours."

His jaw tightened at what she left unsaid. "I have my work to keep me busy." He'd discovered that laboring from dawn until dusk was the only way to keep his mind from being consumed by the enormous tragedy that had taken place four years earlier.

"I'm proud of that, too." She squeezed his wrists. "We couldn't have built all of this without you. The barns, the fences, and the herds." She tipped her head back to gaze fondly up at him. "My boys look up to you more than you'll ever know. If you ever need or want anything from us, all you have to do is ask."

"You pay me more than enough, ma'am." Plus, all six Ford brothers had helped construct his cabin and barn in return for him swinging a hammer to raise their homes and outbuildings. All the boys, except for Jameson, lived in their own cabins on the property.

"You know I wasn't talking about money. I love you like you're my own, Ethan."

"And I love you for saying that, ma'am." He waited for her to continue, sensing there was something else she needed to get off her chest.

"I hope that means you plan to stay." A wrinkle formed in the middle of her sun-kissed brow. "We're your family in every way that counts, and El Vaquero is your home now."

His lips twitched. "I'm glad you're in no hurry to get rid of me, because I wasn't planning on leaving." He couldn't believe she'd wasted any energy worrying about something so unlikely to happen.

"Good, because I won't give you up without a fight." She gave a decided nod, looking visibly relieved.

He glanced around them, grinning. "I don't see anyone trying to take me away from here."

"Maybe not at the moment, but there will be. My boys traveled quite a distance and went to a lot of trouble to recruit you." Her lips twisted. "It's only a matter of time before some big rancher tries to recruit you back. Your services are in great demand, Ethan Vasquez."

He smiled at her affectionately. "It's good to be wanted." He wasn't sure why that fact had her so worried. He was more than content to continue riding for the Ford stables. He would've never bought property and built a cabin on it if he hadn't intended to stick around. He believed in the work that the Fords were doing and enjoyed being a part of pioneering a town.

"You'll be getting other offers soon, and not all of them are the business sort." She stepped back, running a hand over her salt-and-pepper hair. "If Jameson and Keegan get what they want, there will soon be females all across this town batting their eyelashes nonstop at y'all."

Ah. We are back to that topic again. "I reckon there's no point in worrying about it until it happens." Her sons had yet to reveal how they intended to fill their small but growing community with females, and Ethan wasn't holding his breath. They were cowpokes, same as him. Their expertise was in the livestock business, not in the matchmaking business.

"I can't help worrying about you, Ethan. I worry about all of my boys."

"Appreciate that, ma'am." It meant the world to him that she'd included him in her statement.

"I just want to see you happy — all of you. Naturally, that includes finding you suitable wives."

Hold up there, little filly! Ethan jolted and released her hands. "I had a wife, and I'm not on the lookout for another one just yet." A man could only handle so much heartache, and he wasn't convinced that a town as new as theirs was a place for a woman. Not the young, marriageable ones, at any rate. He and the Fords lived too far away from the nearest apothecaries and midwives, among other important services.

Paloma gave a long, drawn-out sigh. "You weren't meant to be alone, my precious boy. Not forever. None of us were."

"Yet here we are, ma'am. You and me both." He hated bringing up her widowed status, not that it was a fair comparison. She was surrounded by men daily, several of which had made no secret about the fact that they'd be standing in line the moment she was ready to court again.

"Oh, Ethan! All you have to do is look around you to see my quiver is full. I have sons who will give me grandsons and granddaughters. I have loved and been loved. I have a lifetime of happy memories and no regrets. And that, my son, is what I want for you." She stabbed her finger against his chest.

He reached up to place his hand over hers. "So, you want me to get married," he said carefully, his gaze narrowing on her bronze features.

"I do, when the time is right." Her eyes brimmed with motherly concern and adoration. "I want to see you happy again." When he started to protest, she shook her head. "Granted, you've found peace after the tragedies, and you are content with your work here, but it's not the same as being happy. I want more for you than what you have right now, Ethan. Please don't be angry with me for saying that. It's what every mother wants for her brood."

Her words, though hard to hear, touched him with her earnestness. "I am not angry with you." He was unable to imagine being angry with her. "I just fear it's too risky for me to wed again so soon. This town is no more ready than the last one was for what happened to my family." Following a difficult pregnancy that had kept his wife bedridden, he'd watched her suffer through the pangs of childbirth, only to lose both her and the babe in the end. He would never forget the delicate, paper-thin bodies he'd placed together in a grave. He would also never forgive himself for bringing them into the wilderness, so far away from the medicinal services to be had in the bigger towns.

"I think you're forgetting about why I get called into El Gato and the surrounding towns so often, my love." She slid her hands up to his shoulders, scowling fiercely at him. "My skills as a midwife are in great demand in these mountain towns. It is my hope that they will soon be in demand in our town as well."

He glanced away, his jaw working. "I have not forgotten what you do."

"Then believe me when I say this. The next time you wed, you will not have to endure what you endured before."

"I believe you. I still don't feel ready to wed again, ma'am." She might as well know the truth. He didn't wish to give her false hopes in his direction.

"Just think about what I've said, my precious boy." Instead of waiting for an answer, she leaned in to rest her head against his chest. "As Bo Stanley reminds us from the pulpit every Sunday, the best is yet to come. I truly believe that."

Ethan had never considered himself to be a religious man, but he awkwardly patted her back, mulling over her words. The discovery that she was worried about him was troubling. He must have gotten careless along the way, allowing her to sense the grief he tried to keep buried. He'd never intended to cause her such distress.

He bent to kiss the top of her head. She smelled of good things, like wheat flour and spices from the kitchen with an underlying hint of rosewater. For some reason, it triggered the memories of his short-lived marriage and brought them flooding back — having someone to converse and laugh with, someone to share the events of his day with, someone to hold at night. Sure, he missed those things during those rare moments that he allowed himself to think and feel. He mostly avoided doing so.

"I will think about what you said," he assured the woman in his arms quietly. She'd taken the time to draw him aside and mother him. The least he could do was listen and appreciate the fact that she cared.

Her arms momentarily tightened around him. "And don't forget the first part of what I said. You're family now, and I don't want you to leave. Ever!" She spat out the last word so fiercely that he chuckled.

"You're a good woman, Paloma Ford. That's why I love you so much."

There were tears in her eyes as she let him go. "Come!" She beckoned him to follow her. "Breakfast is waiting."

As he followed her into the dining room, she scolded, "Breakfast awaits you in this house every morning. I wish you'd show up more often." The room was flickering with candlelight from a row of wall sconces on either side of the table.

His stomach growled at the delicious scents swirling through the air. More than biscuits and gravy were set out on the long farmhouse table. There were also eggs, bacon, and flapjacks. It was a veritable feast!

"Took you long enough!" Jameson's angular features twisted into mock outrage from the head of the table. Keegan was sitting to his left. The empty spot to his right was for his ma.

"You can say that again." Keegan zinged a biscuit at him.

Ethan caught it with one hand and took a seat at the end of the bench nearest the doorway.

"How in the blazes did they talk you into joining us?" The youngest Ford brother, Lance, scooted over to make more room for him. Like his older brothers, the eighteen-year-old was dark-haired, tanned, and wiry. He was also the most outspoken of the bunch.

"Language," his mother admonished, taking her place by Jameson. Carlton, Redding, and Chevy shared her bench, while Lance and Ethan shared Keegan's.

"Yes, ma'am." Lance ducked his head. However, it bobbed right back up. "I reckon you showed up to hear about the first females coming to town and to draw—" A kick from under the table not only bought his silence but had him reaching down to rub his ankle.

The kick told Ethan two things. Number one, the brothers were, in fact, up to something. Number two, it involved him, which couldn't be good.

"First things first," Jameson droned. "Let us say grace." His deadpan expression further supported Ethan's suspicions that the brothers were up to no good.

Everyone bowed their heads while Jameson gave a quick blessing over the food. Then they dug in.

For the next several minutes, the only sounds in the room were silverware clinking against plates and requests to pass seconds of one dish or another.

Ethan finished first, since it was his second breakfast. He half rose from the bench, pretending he was about to leave. "Thank you for breakfast, ma'am." He nodded his head respectfully at Paloma.

"Not so fast!" Jameson laid down his fork and sat back in his chair.

Here it comes. Ethan gave him a look of mock surprise. "I'd best mosey on to the stables, don't you think?"

"No need to rush," Jameson responded in a deceptively smooth voice. "I kept the night crew on patrol a little longer to leave us time to discuss another matter."

"Oh?" Ethan took his time returning to the bench, purposefully keeping his tall frame poised for flight.

"It's an important matter that requires all family members

present, plus a few of the other townsfolk who will be here shortly."

As if on cue, there was a clattering of footsteps against the porch planks, then a knock on the door.

Jameson nodded at Chevy. "How about you do the honors and bring them inside?"

Ethan watched the doorway in curiosity and wasn't overly surprised to see Bo Stanley and Gray Clanton step into the room.

Bo was the newest settler the Fords had brought into their fold — a minister, of all people. Ethan hadn't been expecting the Ford's to open a church so soon, especially in a town with a population of fifty or so men. However, their mother had insisted it was the best way to keep crime down and property disputes at a minimum.

"Morning, preacher!" Ethan rose to extend a hand to him.

"Morning!" Bo shook his hand while casting a hungry look at the table. "Smells mighty good in here." He was a mountain man through-and-through, right down to the coonskin cap sweeping from his brow. Like a lot of men in town, he didn't bother to shave often. His reddish-brown hair dragged his collar, and his sun-streaked beard bushed around his cheeks and chin, nearly hiding his mouth.

"Please join us!" Mrs. Ford waved the two men to the table.

Lance crowded even closer to Keegan to make room on the bench. Ethan chose to remain standing since he'd already eaten. Otherwise, there was no way both Bo and Gray would've fit on the bench. Not to mention he really did need to scoot out of the house soon.

Gray Clanton silently followed behind Bo. He managed the stables. Anything having to do with the horses on Ford Ranch was his business. He fed and watered them, brushed them down, tended their injuries, saddle-broke the wild ones the Fords' captured, and made sure the entire stable of horses was properly rotated through the brothers' various journeys and patrols.

Jameson and Keegan had convinced him to leave a profitable livery business behind in a much larger town. A cowboy in his late forties or early fifties, Gray probably wasn't earning more here than there. However, there were times that Ethan suspected he'd had other reasons for making the move. Those suspicions became stronger every time Gray laid eyes on Paloma, which he was doing right now.

His piercing silver gaze softened as he nodded at her and silently took his seat. Except when he was training the horses in the ring, he was otherwise a quiet man. He knew his place and never overstepped his position, treating each one of Paloma's sons like princes. However, Jameson and Keegan had quickly come to rely on his wisdom and guidance as the senior member of their crew, something that Ethan was pretty sure hadn't gone unnoticed by their mother.

The color in her cheeks deepened as she met his gaze. "Before I forget, Gray, there are some chopped carrots and apples in a bucket in the kitchen. For the horses, of course. Please don't leave without them."

"Yes, ma'am." He inclined his head respectfully. It had always been this way between them. Paloma made most of the conversation and called him by his first name. He treated her like the lady of the house and always used her proper title.

"Alright, alright, alright!" Jameson clapped his hands like the lord of the manor. "Now that everyone is present and accounted for, let's get this meeting started."

"Meeting!" Lance grimaced. "No one said anything about a boring old meeting. This ain't exactly Sunday morning," he groaned. Receiving another kick under the table, he shot an apologetic look at Bo. "No offense, reverend."

"Offense taken, my friend. I have a few chores around the

church that require an extra set of hands. That can be your penance. That is, assuming your ma can spare you for a few hours this afternoon."

"She can," Mrs. Ford announced cheerfully, "just as soon as he finishes helping Chevy with the field they're turning under."

Chevy, who was two years older than Lance, looked relieved.

Jameson waited until their sidebar conversation ended. Then he rested his clasped hands on the table and leaned closer. "So, here's the situation. Keegan and I have been in negotiations for the past two months with an agency that guarantees they can find willing and able-bodied women to help us settle this town."

Ethan tensed. "What's the catch?" He folded his arms and leaned back against the wall, hoping they weren't talking about emptying out a brothel, prison, or insane asylum.

Keegan snickered. "All we have to do is marry them."

Ethan's jaw dropped. He pushed away from the wall. "Marry them!"

"You heard me. Seeing as most of us were already looking to wed and start a family, I don't see why the arrangement should pose any problems." He spread his hands to take in every male seated at the table. "Except maybe Lance. He's still a bit of a whippersnapper."

Lance tossed a piece of biscuit at him, which Keegan caught and popped into his mouth.

Jameson jumped back into the conversation. "The company we've been communicating with is The Western Moon Agency. They specialize in placing mail-order brides in the smallest, hardest to reach, most remote towns in the west." He grinned. "I think El Vaquero more than qualifies for that description." Then his expression grew serious. "When we agreed to settle this town together, I think we all envisioned a place that would eventually be filled with families, did we not?"

After a pregnant pause, in which the men seated glanced warily around the table at each other, heads slowly started to nod.

A mail-order bride agency. If that doesn't beat all! Ethan had heard about such things, though it had always sounded like something out of a storybook — picking a bride from the qualities she listed in her application and marrying her the moment she arrived in town.

He had so many questions, he hardly knew where to start, so he settled for the most obvious. "Where in tarnation is this agency going to find candidates that meet our requirements? Any women traveling this far into the wilderness are going to need strong domestic skills. It wouldn't hurt for them to know a thing or two about farming and caring for livestock, too."

"That's easy." Jameson met his gaze squarely. "They advertise in newspapers all over the country. Since the war depleted a lot of towns of their fighting age men, cowboys like us are actually in great demand at the moment." He puffed out his chest, preening mockingly. "According to the mail-order bride agency's proxy representative, that is."

"How do we sign up?" Chevy waved a hand in the air, as if volunteering.

Ethan noted his mother giving her oldest son a faint head shake, leading him to believe she considered Chevy to be in the same whippersnapper category as her youngest son.

"I think it would be wise to draw straws," Keegan interjected hastily. "We'll pick one man to try out the agency's services and see how they work before the rest of us throw our hats into the ring."

"Proceed with caution, eh?" Bo Stanley nodded his approval. "I like the sound of that."

"Does that mean you're in, sir?" Keegan retorted with a smirk.

"Eh, why not? I'm not getting any younger."

"Younger!" Gray Clanton exploded, straightening in his seat. He usually listened quietly and rarely joined in their conversations, but not today. "I reckon that comment was aimed at the oldest fellow at the table."

Bo's eyes twinkled merrily. "As a matter of fact, it was. That means you should draw a straw, too, old chap."

Gray shook his head in bemusement and grew silent again, shooting a quick glance at Mrs. Ford.

She was frowning in thought and didn't quite meet his gaze.

Interesting. Ethan wondered if he'd been wrong about the attraction prickling between the two of them, since Gray hadn't spoken up to withdraw from the game of straws.

Jameson shifted in his seat. "Is there any man present who doesn't wish to draw a straw?"

Ethan could feel a vein ticking in his jaw. The temptation to raise his hand was strong. However, Paloma's pleading gaze met his.

"Very well." Jameson put his hands behind his back and brought them back in front of him. His fists were full of straws. Standing, he held them out to Keegan first. "We'll draw our straws first. Then we'll look at the same time."

Glancing around the crowded dining room table, Ethan was amazed at how many grown men were willing to let a simple game decide something so monumental about their future. Then again, he was playing along, too.

Beneath the hawk eye of his mother, Jameson passed over both Chevy and Lance. Neither brother seemed all that perturbed by it. By the time he reached the corner where Ethan was standing, there were only two straws left. "You look like a thundercloud," he taunted in a low voice. "If this is too much adventure for a fellow of your advanced years—"

With a snarling sound, Ethan snatched one of the straws from his hand.

Jameson waved the final piece of straw in the air. It was one of the longest ones in the room. "Clearly, I am not getting married first. Who is?"

Every man held up his straw.

Gray Clanton eyed the shortest one in his hand with a grave expression. "I'll confess, I was expecting the honor to go to one of you younger fellows." Though he often looked at Paloma when he was speaking, this time he did not.

As hoots and cheers of congratulations erupted, Ethan shot a speculative glance at the woman he loved like a mother. She'd grown very still and pale.

The suspicions he'd harbored for months were finally verified. She had feelings for Gray Clanton. He clenched his jaw. *Whereas I have a block of stone where my heart used to be.*

"I'll go first," he heard himself saying.

The cheering jangled to a halt.

"I don't recall any rules against trading straws, so here's mine if you want it." He held out his longer straw to Gray Clanton, half hoping he would refuse it.

This time, Gray Clanton did venture a peek at Paloma. Her lips were parted and trembling as she waited for him to decide. Without another word, the senior cowboy reached for Ethan's straw.

As Ethan accepted the shorter straw, emotions he hadn't felt in a long time spewed through his gut — excitement, fear, and the tiniest curl of hope. Though he might not be capable of loving again, Mrs. Ford was right. He was a lonely man, one who desperately still wanted a family of his own despite everyone and everything he'd lost.

She shot off the bench and flew in his direction to deliver a fierce hug. "Thank you," she murmured. Then she stepped back to give him a tremulous smile. "You're getting married," she sighed. "My lands! You're getting married, son."

Married. He repeated the word in his head to help it sink in. There was nothing quite like having one's biscuits and gravy served up with the promise of being wed soon.

Chapter 3: Dramatic Entrance

ANNABELLE

Sensing that she was being followed, Annabelle increased her pace. It wasn't easy walking fast along the edge of the cobblestone street while wearing a corset and carrying a black travel bag in each hand. Though she no longer possessed many belongings, it was still heavy to carry them all at the same time.

Thankfully, she'd memorized the address of the law office listed at the bottom of the advert. Apparently, J.R. Hubert & Sons would be acting in proxy for The Western Moon Agency.

Every so often, she glanced over her shoulder but saw nothing amiss. Nevertheless, the feeling that she was being watched did not fade until she stepped inside the law office.

A woman with her hair pulled severely back glanced over the top of her spectacles as the front door jingled, announcing Annabelle's arrival. She gave Annabelle's faded silk gown a nose-wrinkling perusal, leaving her feeling like something was wrong with her outfit.

"I presume you are here in response to the advert for mail-order brides," the woman announced crisply.

"Yes, ma'am."

"Have a seat." She nodded at the chair in front of her desk.

"I am Hettie Goodwin, the head secretary of this office, and I will be assisting you with your application."

"Pleased to meet you, ma'am." It was a relief to finally set down her bags, one on either side of her chair.

The woman pushed her spectacles higher on her nose and fixed Annabelle with an assessing stare. "Name, please." She picked up a pen, dipped it in her ink bottle, and held it over a form. There was no wedding band on her finger.

"Annabelle Lane, ma'am."

The woman started to write. Despite the sultry temperature outside, she was wearing a high-necked black gown, a clear sign she was in mourning.

"Is your family aware of your desire to become a mail-order bride?"

They would roll over in their graves if they did. Annabelle caught her breath. "Regrettably, I no longer have a family. The war..." Her voice broke, and she was unable to continue.

"I understand." Ms. Goodwin's expression lost some of its severity. "I am all too familiar with the costs of war." Though she did not elaborate, Annabelle could only assume she'd lost someone very dear.

"Your age?" the secretary inquired next.

"Three and twenty, ma'am."

"And your reason for wanting to become a mail-order bride?" Her voice was infused with undeniable disapproval.

Oh, dear! Annabelle's instincts told her that Ms. Goodwin would know if she was lying, so she settled for the truth. "I have lost everyone and everything I hold dear, minus a few friends with whom I am currently sharing a boarding house room. We are dirt poor, exhausted, and barely making our rent payment despite working every daylight hour seven days per week. Though it sounds like a horrendous existence, I was reasonably content with it until a few hours ago. That was when the rogue who purchased my family's home informed me that my dearly departed father left this world indebted to him. He informed me that I had two options for settling the debt — by either marrying him and giving him an heir, or by dealing with the debt collectors he will send my way tomorrow."

Ms. Goodwin's mouth fell open as she listened to Annabelle's sorry tale. "Utterly barbaric!" she gasped at its conclusion, dipping her pen again. She rapidly completed the rest of the form. "Though Mr. Hubert is out of town, I am confident he will approve of what I am about to do."

Hope bloomed in Annabelle's chest. "Which is...?"

"I am placing you with a groom, of course." She continued to write. "A good man, from the sound of his application and his attached letter of reference. With respect to time, I'll give you the short version of them. Mr. Ethan Vasquez is a range rider in a very small, very remote mountain community in Texas."

Texas? Oh, my! Annabelle had heard stories about the wild, untamed canyons and deserts of the enormous state. However, small and remote was exactly what she was looking for at the moment — the farther from Atlanta, the better. "It sounds like the perfect placement for me," she murmured. Her heart raced with a mixture of apprehension and excitement. *This is really happening!*

Ms. Goodwin sniffed. "It can barely be called a town, mind you. They boast a population of approximately fifty men and one woman. However, they are anxious to change that number. It is their fondest hope that you will be the first of many mail-order brides who agree to settle there."

Annabelle hoped it meant that the friends she was leaving behind would stand a chance of following her to the same place. "Where do I sign?" she asked simply.

Within a handful of minutes, Ms. Goodwin had the

paperwork completed and a hackney hailed to carry them to the train station.

"It is so kind of you to come along," Annabelle breathed. Though she was grateful for the woman's presence, she'd not been expecting the luxury of an escort.

"Mr. Hubert has a special account at the train station," Ms. Goodwin informed her primly. "It is best if I am the one to purchase your ticket. Mr. Vasquez has graciously provided a small travel allowance as well." She handed Annabelle a sealed white envelope. "Normally, I would suggest you invest in a new gown or fill a trousseau, but there is no time for such things. Fortunately, you seem to be in possession of a lovely wardrobe already."

Annabelle spared a wry glance at her gown. Though the blue silk was fading, there was no hiding the superior cut of it. "Thank you for the funds. Without them, I would be traveling penniless." She hastily deposited the envelope in her reticule.

A commotion in the street to their left had their heads spinning.

"Stop the hackney!" a man shouted. "We'll double whatever they are paying you."

Their driver snorted and cracked his whip over his team of horses. "I think not, you rapscallions!" Tossing the two women seated behind him an apologetic look, he announced, "Hold on tight, ladies. We're about to pick up speed."

Ms. Goodwin grasped the side of the hackney with one hand and her hat in the other. "Who are they?" she gasped.

"Nothing more than cockroaches! Every last one of them. They pretend to hail a ride, then rob the driver blind."

Annabelle shuddered at their boldness to operate in broad daylight.

"Exactly, how m-many are there?" Ms. Goodwin stammered.

"Two at the moment, but they are part of a much larger

group. Never you fear, madams, I shall get you safely to the train station and happily report them to the first deputy we encounter."

"If this is my fault, I am sorry." Annabelle hissed to Ms. Goodwin in dismay. "My deadline to pay the loan was not supposed to be until tomorrow. I never dreamt they would pursue me so soon."

"The driver seems to know who these scoundrels are. Thus, we cannot assume they are after you, my dear." Ms. Goodwin spoke through white lips, clearly trying to offer reassurance, but Annabelle knew better.

"God speed," she whispered, as the driver relentlessly drove his horses onward. The wheels of the hackney clattered and skid across the cobblestones.

"Almost there!" he shouted.

How he reached the base of the train platform without running into another wagon would forever be a mystery to Annabelle. She was simply grateful that he did.

"I have an idea," Ms. Goodwin muttered as they scrambled up the steps of the platform. Each of them was carrying one of Annabelle's travel bags. "It will require a little maneuvering, mind you." She gave Annabelle's gown a lengthy once-over as they jogged into the train station. Then she beckoned her to follow as she cut to the front of the line.

"Hey, lady!" someone protested behind them.

Ms. Goodwin paid them no mind. She slapped a card down on the cabinet at the attendant's window. "We request a private appointment for the law office of J.R. Hubert & Sons. Immediately."

Annabelle watched in amazement as the sandy-haired clerk gave her a nervous nod and hopped down from his stool. He pulled open the iron door next to his window marked *Authorized Staff Only,* and ushered them through. They arrived at an inner sanctum without windows. A long conference table surrounded by richly upholstered chairs graced the room. The surrounding walls were covered in dark wooden panels.

"One of our managers will be with you shortly, ma'am." The clerk politely inclined his head at Ms. Goodwin and took his leave.

Annabelle watched their exchange with envy. There was a time when her family's name had commanded similar respect.

"We need to make this quick." Ms. Goodwin unbuttoned the neck of her dress. "You'll wear my dress out of this room, and I will wear yours. It's not a perfect plan, but it should buy you some time."

Annabelle frowned at the realization that the law secretary believed the ruffians were indeed after them. "Aren't you in mourning, ma'am?"

A faint smile stole over the woman's mouth. "I believe with all of my heart that my dearly departed brother would approve of what I am doing. He gave his all for the cause of freedom. The least I can do to honor his sacrifice is to help one innocent girl escape the clutches of a few hoodlums in Atlanta." Her smile widened. "Assuming you do not mind traveling across the country in the somber shade of black."

"Not at all. To be honest, it's probably safer. I wish I had been the one to think of it." Annabelle knew she was babbling, but it helped ease her tightly coiled nerves.

They hastily switched dresses and helped each other button and tweak them into place. Both were panting by the time the task was completed.

"I'll never forget your kindness, ma'am," she added breathlessly.

Ms. Goodwin pinned her with a warning look. "I am happy to help, but the rest is up to you. You must keep your head down and not look back, no matter how tempting it is."

Through a complicated exchange that Annabelle did not

fully understand, she was next placed on a Pullman sleeper car. "You have a long journey ahead." Ms. Goodwin glanced around the fast filling train car. "Your bench during the day will be converted to a sleeping berth at night. Though I am sure you are accustomed to much greater luxuries, this is the best I can do for you."

"Good gracious!" Annabelle stared in amazement at the woman. "These are far grander accommodations than I was expecting. I thank you from the bottom of my heart." Not in her wildest imagination had she thought a range rider would be capable of coming up with the funds for a Pullman car.

Ms. Goodwin leaned in to give her a quick hug. "God be with you, Miss Lane."

"And you," Annabelle said softly. "May His grace ease your heartache and comfort you during this time of loss."

"That is a prayer that applies to both of us. Amen and amen." With a final pat on Annabelle's shoulder, the law secretary wove her way up the crowded aisle and exited the car.

Annabelle watched her progress across the busy train platform as she waved down another hackney. She jolted in her seat as two men dressed in black converged on Ms. Goodwin. She shrieked and waved her reticule at them. Her theatrics swiftly attracted a small crowd of onlookers.

Men from the crowd stepped forward to drag the two rogues away from her. As the train hooted a warning of its pending departure, one of the rogues shot a dark look at the very car Annabelle was sitting in. A stunned expression spread across his features. Gesturing wildly at his companion, they simultaneously broke away from those holding them captive and raced back up the steps of the train platform.

Horrified at how quickly they'd guessed what Ms. Goodwin had done, Annabelle shrank away from the window. The train started to roll forward.

Please, God, let it be too late to open the door!

The two ruffians in black ran alongside the train, beating at the windows.

Something inside of Annabelle snapped. She was mindlessly exhausted, and the only penny to her name was what had been sent to her by the perfect stranger she would soon wed. She was leaving behind the only people she knew in the only city she'd ever lived in, rendering her a woman with precious little left to lose. If the two cowards on the other side of her window thought they were in the position to intimidate her any further, they were sorely mistaken.

Leaning back toward the window, she tipped her forehead against it. Lifting her hand in a fluttering wave, she shot the nearest rogue a triumphant smile.

He stumbled forward a step, shocked by her boldness. It turned out to be an unfortunate move on his part since he'd reached the edge of the platform.

Watching him topple off of it was one of the most satisfying things Annabelle had experienced in months. She settled deeper in her seat, laughing until she cried.

Two weeks later

THE WHEELS OF THE TRAIN SQUEALED AGAINST THE tracks as it slowed for its final stop into El Gato. Annabelle checked to ensure that her copy of the mail-order bride contract was still safe inside her reticule, along with the precious envelope of money. They were. According to Ms. Goodwin, her groom would sign his section of the contract upon her arrival. Or soon after. After reaching El Gato, Annabelle would take a stagecoach the rest of the way to the hometown of her groom-to-be. He lived in El Vaquero, a newly established mountain community, which she could only presume did not yet boast its own railroad spur.

Ethan Vasquez. Annabelle inwardly repeated the name of her intended as she stared out the window at the acres of wild mountain laurel. The purple blooms stretched all the way to the distant mountains where she was headed.

She would soon be wed to a range rider, a man who patrolled the countryside for any sign of danger while herding cattle. His job sounded scads more exciting than the life of drudgery she'd been leading in Atlanta. She'd just about worked her fingers to the bone as a laundress and seamstress. It had taken a full two weeks aboard the train to grow out her chipped fingernails. Her calluses were very much still intact, though.

She wasn't certain that she would ever get rid of them. Mr. Ethan Vasquez desired a wife who possessed both an adventurous spirit and strong domestic skills. *Ugh!* It honestly sounded as if he'd taken his list of requirements straight from the advert. It left her wondering what else he was looking for in a wife. A companion? A friend? Someone to bear his children? She blushed at the thought. Did he even want children?

It was way too bad there'd been so little time for questions up front during her brief appointment with Ms. Goodwin, not that it would have altered her decision to travel west. She was fortunate to have boarded her train before Mr. Featherfall's debt collectors caught up to her. It was despicable the way he'd sent them after her prematurely. She could only hope he wasn't despicable enough to send his goons this far from Georgia to continue hounding her.

The train finished squealing its way into the station. As a precaution, Annabelle had changed into a fresh dress. Not only was Ms. Goodwin's black gown the last thing her followers had seen her in, it also happened to be her wedding day. For this reason, she'd donned a gown of grass green cotton speckled with tiny white rosettes. A straw hat was tied beneath her chin with a ribbon the shade of charcoal. At the last minute, she decided to leave her hair down. She had the start of a headache and didn't need a pile of pins to make it worse. Something told her that a rough and tough range rider like Mr. Vasquez wouldn't be overly concerned about which way her hair was styled.

A lone stagecoach was waiting at the base of the platform steps when she disembarked from the train. Hoping it was hers, she hurried toward it with her two travel bags. At the sight of her, the driver hopped down from his perch and tossed her bags on top. She thanked him and turned to climb inside the coach. One of the two gentlemen already seated inside leaned out to assist her up.

"I appreciate your kindness." She beamed a grateful smile at him. He was a dapper man of middling years in a tweed suit and a black top hat. Sitting across from him was a cowboy in faded denim trousers and a Stetson. Annabelle eyed the twin holsters he had strapped to his belt, wishing she owned a set.

He followed her gaze. "Do you like to hunt, ma'am?"

She shook her head ruefully. "I'm afraid I haven't had the pleasure in a while." Once upon a time, her father had given her a series of shooting lessons, but it felt like a lifetime ago.

He drew out one of the pistols and twirled it expertly.

She watched him with interest.

"Would you like to try it?" He offered it to her with the barrel pointed down.

"What I would like, more than anything, is to own one," she confessed, accepting the empty gun. "Will you sell it to me?" When she attempted to give it a twirl, it wasn't near as difficult as she expected.

"You're a natural." He eyed her admiringly. "Might I ask who you're aiming to plug a hole into?"

"No one." She gave him a tight smile. On a burst of inspiration, she decided to test out the name of her intended to see if either of her travel companions had heard of him. "I'm simply trying to make it in one piece to El Vaquero, where I shall wed Mr. Ethan Vasquez."

The cowboy's mouth fell open. "Lady, if what you say is true, you're more than welcome to the pistol. All I want in return is for you to put in a good word for me with him."

She drew her eyebrows together. "A good word for what, exactly?"

"To come work for your husband, that's what!" He shot her an incredulous look, as if unable to believe her ignorance. "He's the best range rider in all of Texas. Ain't no hombres from here to the border willing to cross him. What I could learn from a fellow like him!"

"If you throw in a few bullets, it's a deal." She hated pressing him for more, but an empty gun would be of no use to her if trouble came knocking.

Without hesitation, he dug six or seven bullets from his pocket and handed them to her.

She eagerly accepted them. "What name should I recommend to Mr. Vasquez?"

"Garth." The cowboy extended his hand to her. "Garth Swingler."

A pop of gunfire in the distance had them diving for the window to see what was happening outside.

"Huh!" Garth pushed his Stetson farther back on his head. "Unless I'm reading this wrong, we're about to be waylaid by a pair of highwaymen."

Annabelle's insides quaked. "Please assure me you're jesting."

"Sorry, lady." He shook his head gravely at her. "Would you like me to load your pistol for you?"

"No. I think I remember how." Her hands shook as she

did the deed and cocked the pistol. "Are they still out there?" she inquired nervously.

"Out there and closing in," he affirmed, pulling yet another pistol from his boot. Giving them a twirl, he rested the barrels on the windowsill. "Won't be long now 'til they're in firing range." He sounded more excited than fearful.

Looking resigned, the other gentleman produced a handgun and positioned himself at the opposite window. "I'm getting too old for this," he grumbled.

Annabelle peeped around Garth and shivered at the sight of two outlaws riding their way. Their faces were covered from the nose down with black kerchiefs. "What do we do next?" She had no experience dealing with highwaymen. It was the stuff of storybooks.

Garth shrugged. "Shoot back, if we have to. If he's smart, our driver will make tracks to El Vaquero. With any luck, Vasquez and his crew will help get us out of this mess."

As the shots grew closer, the stagecoach horses panicked and took off at a gallop. Annabella braced her boots against the floor to remain in her seat while gripping her pistol with both hands. The stagecoach careened along the narrow path so swiftly that it was a wonder its wheels didn't loosen and fly right off.

Garth and the older gentleman fired an occasional shot back at the bandits. It was enough to keep the riders and their horses hanging back out of firing range. The two riders stayed hot on their trail, however, for the next half mile or so.

"I see something," Annabelle announced excitedly as she peered over Garth's hunkered down figure to see what lay ahead. "A town, I think. I see a church with a steeple."

Despite the desperateness of their circumstances, she was charmed by the tiny white church, more than a little amazed by the fact that a town with only fifty people had seen fit to build a church so quickly. They certainly had their priorities straight.

She hollered out the window to the driver, "Get us to the church!"

He nodded without turning around and kept driving.

Garth eyed her in amusement. "Way to take charge, Mrs. Soon-to-be Vasquez!"

She figured she'd made it too far across the country to give up now. "I'm going to make it to the church on time for my wedding if I have to jump from this stagecoach while it's still moving." She had no idea how she'd retrieve her luggage stored on the rooftop, but she would find a way. She had no wish to lose the rest of her wardrobe. It was all she had left of her former life. There were a few embroidered linens that had once belonged to her mother. Plus, her father's watch was tucked down the side of one of the travel bags.

"I like your spirit." Garth shook his head in admiration. "What I don't like is the thought of you jumping out of this rig alone. Without a partner to cover your back, I don't see how you'll ever make it inside the church before..."

Before I take a bullet. She made a face at him to let him know she understood. However, the sight of the church had emboldened her. Surely, they would find sanctuary there, if only they could make it inside in time.

"Tell you what," the cowboy drawled. "How about I jump at the same time as you, and we make the run together?"

The other gentleman looked at them like they were crazy. "I'll give you as much cover fire as I can from right here, but don't ask me to join you. My bones are too old for that."

"It's a sound plan." Swinging to his feet, Garth clapped a hand on the man's shoulder. He had to stoop to move across the stagecoach beneath the short ceiling.

As Annabelle shimmied the top half of her slender frame

out the window, he lunged forward to hold her steady. "What you are doing?"

"Retrieving my bags. All of my earthly possessions are up top. I don't wish to leave them behind."

Snorting out a laugh, the cowboy tugged her away from the window. "I'll do it."

She lifted her chin. "I didn't ask you to."

He jutted his chin right back at her. "Unless you have any experience jumping from moving vehicles…" he taunted.

She did not. "Do you?"

"Sure do. That makes me the better choice for going up."

"No, it doesn't," she cried. "It's my choice to risk my hide for my belongings, not yours."

"On the contrary, Ethan Vasquez will never hire me if I let you do that, so step aside, ma'am. Hold tight and don't jump until I say to." Without waiting for her answer, he twisted his lithe body through the window opening and scrambled like a monkey to the rooftop.

More shots sounded outside.

Gritting her teeth, Annabelle dashed back to the other window to gauge how close the two horsemen were getting.

Good gracious! They were probably close enough now for their bullets to reach Garth. Though it had been years since she last fired a gun, she raised her pistol and shot off a round. Both Garth and the older gentleman fired their pistols at the same time.

One of the horses reared up, pawing the air frantically and dumped his rider to the ground. Then he took off running in the opposite direction.

One down. One to go. Annabelle had no way of knowing which bullet had done the deed, but a sense of glee stole over her. It felt good to fight back.

The second rider flanked wide to the left during the final stretch of their race to the church. Scruffy grasses and wildflowers flew past the windows. Unsure of what the bandit was up to, Annabelle's biggest fear was that he was trying to get a better angle on Garth.

"Oh, no you don't!" she seethed, clenching her jaw. It was her fault Garth was up there, and she didn't plan to leave him unprotected. The terrain ahead narrowed as the horses pounded their hooves ever closer to their destination.

At her best estimate, the horse and his rider would be back in firing range in three, two, one...

Today was the first time she'd ever shot at anything other than ducks and geese, but a target was a target. She fired her pistol again. The rider jerked in his saddle and reached for his knee. Red seeped from beneath his hand. "Got him!" she chortled.

The stagecoach soon outpaced the wounded rider. He hollered for his team to slow down as they reached the entrance of the pass.

Annabelle leaned out the window again. "We got them, sir. All is well."

Though he slowed the horses to a trot, he kept them rolling at a decent clip.

"We're almost there!" Garth slid back inside the coach, grinning from ear to ear. "That's some mighty fine shooting over there, Miss."

"Annabelle," she supplied. "Annabelle Lane." At least until she became Annabelle Vasquez.

"It's been my pleasure traveling alongside the brave wife of Ethan Vasquez." His voice was so admiring that she felt a flush rise to her cheeks.

"I was grateful for your assistance, partner." It was the most excitement she'd ever had. Exhilaration pumped through her veins.

"We're no more than a minute from the church." Garth pointed ahead.

Annabelle squinted through the sunlight to follow his arm. The simple one-story church was even more charming up close.

"And here comes our second wave of trouble," the other gentleman warned from the window. He'd not ceased his vigil of what was happening behind the stagecoach.

"Oh, dear!" Annabelle shot a worried look at Garth.

"Same plan as before," he assured firmly. "I'll toss down your bags. You wait until I say jump."

She nodded, her heart pounding anew as she watched for her bags to hit the ground.

It didn't happen. Garth leaped down from the roof instead, jogging to a halt with her two bags in hand.

Gasping at the devil-may-care stunt, she threw open the stagecoach door, held up her skirts, and leaped after him. By some miracle, she managed to land on her feet. It took a few stutter steps to right herself.

"I didn't say jump yet," Garth growled, tossing the bags in her direction. He drew his pistols and started firing both of them at the same time. "We're surrounded," he cried without looking at her again. "Run!"

She picked up the handles of her bags and dashed for the church. Men crawled out from behind boulders and Joshua trees, swarming toward the church yard like ants. They were still some distance away. It was difficult to determine if they were close enough to shoot.

A man with a dark, bushy beard appeared in the open doorway of the church. He lifted a rifle and added his firepower to the fray, giving Garth the opportunity to jog backwards and catch up to Annabelle.

"Get inside!" the bearded man bellowed.

Annabelle ducked beneath his burly arm, panting, to drop her bags within the safety of the walls. Garth was close behind her. The bearded man slammed the door shut and bolted it.

"Who are you and what in tarnation is going on?" he thundered as he raced to the nearest window. Propping it open, he crouched behind it, bracing himself for a confrontation.

"I'm so sorry!" Anabelle breathed. "I'm supposed to marry Ethan Vasquez this morning, but we were followed here by those-those..." She pointed to the window, not certain what to call them.

"They're mercenaries," the bearded man snarled. "What could they possibly want from the bride of Ethan Vasquez?"

"I truly do not know," she quavered. "'We thought the stagecoach was about to be robbed, but..."

"But they followed the two of you after you got off." He shook his head in puzzlement. "If that doesn't beat all!"

"I'm clean, and poor as a church mouse to boot," Garth announced. "Ain't no one ever bothered to look twice in my direction before. It has to be you they're after, Miss Annabelle."

"The only man I know who would do something like this is back in Atlanta," she protested. "That's over a thousand miles away."

"A telegram could travel that distance in nothing flat." The bearded man snapped his fingers for emphasis. "I'm Pastor Bo Stanley, by the way, the fellow performing your wedding ceremony."

She gave a sobbing laugh. "I'm not so sure there's going to be a ceremony, Pastor Stanley." It felt like she and Garth had gotten caught in the middle of a war.

"Bo," he corrected. "We don't stand on ceremony around here, and I assure you there *will* be a wedding if Ethan has anything to say about it." He hunkered over his rifle. "Which he will. Ah. There he is now."

Annabelle rushed around the single row of pews in the narrow building in an attempt to peer past his shoulder.

"Hang back, miss," he ordered briskly. "You there, cowboy! Take one of the windows on the other side."

Garth complied, raising both of his pistols in anticipation.

"What can I do? You can't expect me to just stand here," Annabelle cried. Unfortunately, she was out of bullets, so her newly acquired pistol was worthless at the moment.

"Why not?" Bo asked mildly. "It's your wedding day."

"Because it's my groom out there in danger," she seethed, moving to stand at the window down from him.

And there he was.

She caught her breath at the sight of her groom. He was easy to pick out from the others, since he wasn't wearing a cloth tied over his face. A bronze-skinned hulk of a man, he was in desperate need of a shave, but that wasn't even the worst of it. His clothing was torn, his longish black hair was spilling out from beneath his Stetson, and his knees and elbows were bleeding.

"That's Ethan Vasquez?" she gasped. Because of his last name, she'd been expecting a foreigner, not a complete savage.

"The one and only," Bo assured with a chuckle.

"Is that how mountain folks dress for their weddings?" Her voice grew faint.

"Hardly." Bo snorted as he raised his weapon and fired again. "That's how mountain folks dress after they've been in a tussle with a wild animal. Mark my words. That's what he's been up to, and I can guarantee the other critter lost."

She wrinkled her forehead, trying to picture herself trading vows with such a beastly looking man. It was impossible to conjure up such a picture in her head. "How can you be so sure that he bested the other creature?"

"Because he's still alive."

Annabelle shivered as she watched her intended drop to his belly and low-crawl toward the church. Despite her shock at his unkempt appearance, a grudging respect set in. He was brave. She would give him that. Foolish, but brave.

Bullets zinged back and forth over his head as he neared the building.

Bo and Garth fired back at the swarm of bandits. They must have winged a few, because their numbers began to dwindle. She reckoned they were slinking away to tend their wounds.

"Why is he taking such a risk?" she muttered beneath her breath. Ethan Vasquez could have held back and waited out the battle until it was safer for him to approach.

"For you, ma'am," Bo supplied. "Clearly, the bandits aren't the only ones who find you worth fighting for."

It was a tense next several minutes, filled with the volley of gunfire and the occasional shouts of the bandits. By some miracle, Ethan Vasquez finally reached the steps of the porch.

"Unbolt the door!" Bo roared. He continued to fire his weapons without pause.

I reckon you mean me. Annabelle left her post and raced to the front entrance. Her fingers shook as she unbolted the door.

"And stay behind it!"

She yanked it open, and her groom tumbled inside on all fours. The moment he scrambled out of the way, she slammed the door shut.

"Help is on the way!" Garth gave a whoop of delight. "Best leave the door unlocked."

"It's about time!" The man at Annabelle's feet scrambled to his feet. His dark gaze met and held hers for an electrifying moment.

Her knees grew weak. *Good gracious!* This was the man she was supposed to marry? He looked half-wild, and there was so much of him in height and breadth that his presence seemed to fill the room.

"The good guys got the place surrounded," Garth's voice rang with triumph as he shouted updates their way. "You should see them bandits scattering like rodents!"

Moments later, a group of tall, dark-haired, and heavily tanned cowboys strode into the sanctuary. They looked so much alike that they had to be related.

Annabelle dropped Ethan's gaze to examine the newcomers. There were six of them in all. No, wait. There were more. They parted to reveal a petite Hispanic woman they'd been hovering protectively over. Her skirt was layered in colors from every hue of the rainbow. Her blouse was a much simpler white cotton, though it was richly embroidered with roses. Her mostly dark hair was threaded here and there with silver strands. She was accompanied by a middle-aged gentleman in a somber pinstriped suit with frost at his temples.

At the sight of Annabelle's intended, the tiny woman gave a shriek of alarm and flew in his direction. "Ethan! What happened to you?"

"A grizzly bear, ma'am, but I got to him before he could get to the herd. He was after one of the new calves."

"Oh, my precious boy," she sighed, perusing his torn, muddy, and blood-spattered clothing. "And then those ruffians came out of nowhere — on your wedding day, no less." The glance she spared Annabelle was one of utter distress. "I promise you he will look like a different man once he cleans up."

"But you made it, love. That's what matters." The woman returned to fussing over Ethan as he slammed his pistols into their holsters.

"It looks worse than it is. Nothing more than a scratch or two," he assured her as he turned to hold out a hand to Annabelle. "Ethan Vasquez, at your service."

"Annabelle Lane." Despite his faint Spanish accent, his English was good. At least they would have no trouble understanding each other. Swallowing hard, she eyed his hand warily. In addition to the grime, it was mottled with burn scars. She lightly pressed her fingers to his, hoping she wouldn't injure him further. *Only a scratch, my hide!* He was injured. She was sure of it.

He closed his large paw around hers and turned with her to face the platform. "I reckon we should get on with the ceremony if you still wish to be wed. There's no telling when those ruffians will return."

It wasn't a very romantic thing to hear from her groom-to-be. Nevertheless, he was right. If Mr. Featherfall had stooped low enough to hire mercenaries via telegram to drag her back to Atlanta… She stopped, unwilling to let her mind go there. Not on her wedding day.

At Annabelle's silence, Ethan Vasquez added, "It's not too late to change your mind, ma'am. I can have you on the next train out of here, if you prefer."

She shivered at the thought of being chased by bandits all the way back to the depot. Stepping closer to him, she declared, "I'm not sure it's safe to go anywhere right now, sir." Certainly not if Mr. Featherfall was involved in today's shenanigans. The last place she needed to be right now was alone.

Her intended gazed down at her, his dark eyes lighting at her words. "I can't argue that, ma'am." Though his appearance was atrocious, his voice was kind. "I do apologize for not cleaning up before our wedding. It was all I could do to make it here on time."

She gave a shaky laugh. "I arrived in a spray of bullets myself, though I didn't have to wrestle a bear first. I'm in no position to cast judgment."

"Does that mean you still wish to go through with the wedding?"

Wish? No. What she wished was that her parents were still

alive, and that there'd been no need to travel west and wed a complete stranger. She drew a bracing breath and fought the sting of tears. But this wasn't about what she wanted. It was about surviving.

"To be honest, I'd rather take my chances with a man not firing a gun at me," she confessed breathlessly. It was a lame reason to marry, but Ethan Vasquez was clearly the lesser of the evils surrounding her.

A grin stretched his tanned and dusty features, revealing a set of white teeth. "Any idea what those rapscallions wanted from you, Miss Lane?"

She shook her head. "I've never seen them before."

"Of course you haven't. They're hired guns, which means someone paid 'em to come after you."

She raised and lowered her shoulders helplessly. "I only have one enemy in this world that I know of. He claims my dearly departed father owed him a debt and the only way I can settle it is by marrying him."

"A rather ungallant solution."

"I thought so and refused."

"Does he have any proof of the debt?"

"If he does, he has yet to produce it. Regardless, he had me followed to the train station. I presume they were debt collectors, but I am not entirely certain. My train departed before they could get to me."

"I'm glad to hear it." His expression was inscrutable. "Might I ask the sum this man claims you owe him?"

She grimaced and whispered it to him. "He said it was to pay for my mother's medicine before she passed." Every time she repeated it aloud, it sounded even less plausible. To her knowledge, her family had no prior relationship with Mr. Featherfall, nor was he a banker or a money lender by trade.

"It's an odd claim to be sure."

"True." Annabelle made a face. "I reckon it's only fair of

me to ask if you wish to change your mind about the wedding, now that you know the trouble dogging my heels."

He looked amused. "If you knew me better, ma'am, you wouldn't have bothered asking. I am a man of my word." His fingers tightened around hers. "If I seem quiet, it's only because I'm mulling over our dilemma."

Our? Her heart leaped at his words. They were not yet wed, but his hackles were already stirring on her behalf. It was a good sign.

"I own nothing of value, if that is what you're wondering," she continued in a breathy voice. "I lost everything to the war — my parents, my brothers, and my home." Her voice hitched as she recounted her losses. The only way she'd made it this far beyond the string of tragedies was by dwelling on them as little as possible. "I cannot imagine what the bandits want from me," she finished, swallowing hard. "Perhaps, they mistook me for someone else."

"Perhaps." After another long, searching look at her, Ethan Vasquez nodded at Bo Stanley who was bounding up the stairs of the platform to take his place behind the pulpit. "We are ready to be wed."

Chapter 4: State of Disarray
ETHAN

Ethan gazed at his bride-to-be, stunned by his good fortune. *Annabelle.* He repeated her name inside his head, liking the length and cadence of it. She was a far cry from the sturdy country lass he'd been expecting to join him at the altar. Despite her blonde hair being mussed from the gun battle and her dress wrinkled from her travels, she was so beautiful that it was hard to breathe around her.

Her mannerisms were ladylike, her speech was educated, and she was in no small supply of bravery. He couldn't, for the life of him, figure out why such a desirable creature would sign her life away via a mail-order bride contract unless her situation was even more desperate than she was letting on. He intended to get to the bottom of it, and soon.

In the meantime, his instincts were telling him that the woman standing beside him was everything she appeared to be — lovely, afraid, and in urgent need of protection. It was a service he was happy to provide now and in the coming days. Despite the troubles his bride-to-be was carrying on her slender shoulders, she was already fast chasing his loneliness away.

It was way too bad that he'd arrived at the church looking his worst for their first meeting — filthy and bleeding, with his clothing torn in too many places to count. It was a miracle she hadn't taken off running for the train depot after getting an eyeful of him.

Bo Stanley cleared his throat, reclaiming Ethan's attention and making him wonder if the man was doing it to cover a laugh. He was probably never going to hear the last of how bad he looked on his wedding day.

"Dearly beloved," Bo droned, opening his Bible. "We are gathered together to join this man and this woman in holy matrimony."

Ethan only half listened to his friend's opening remarks. He was too busy reveling in the beauty standing beside him. Her green floral gown, though a tad faded, was finely cut. He could easily imagine her whirling around a dance floor in it. The calluses on her fingers, however, were a reminder of the hard times that had hit so many families during the war, especially in the south.

Death and tragedy. They were the great equalizers. The woman at his side had suffered as much as he had, possibly more. His sympathies stirred as she lifted her chin and spoke her vows to him in a clear, firm voice. She was a real lady and a strong one. He pledged his life to her in return, feeling like he'd been handed an enormous gift. It was one he intended to guard, defend, and treasure until the end of his days.

At the conclusion of the ceremony, Bo's voice waxed sly. "I now pronounce you husband and wife. You may kiss your bride."

As Ethan turned to face Annabelle, he could see her shoulders tense. He ever so gently tipped her chin up with two fingers, not wanting to get her dirty. His head descended towards hers, eyes wide open so he could drink her in.

Her eyes were the shade of the bluebells that grew wild all

over the countryside. They were soft and luminous with a tinge of uncertainty that grew to something akin to alarm as his breath tangled with hers.

A split second before their lips touched, she turned her face away. His mouth grazed her cheek instead.

Eh, well, I tried. Though he couldn't blame her for not wanting to get too close to her filthy groom, he heard a few muffled snickers behind him from the Ford brothers. His failure to give his bride a proper kiss was yet another thing he'd be hearing about later. Sometimes it was painful having six brothers.

He schooled his expression as he turned with his bride to face their small audience. As far as he was concerned, the Ford men could smirk and snicker all they wanted. In a few minutes, he would walk out the front door of the church with the most beautiful bride in Texas on his arm. He would get the last laugh.

To his irritation, he was limping as he led Annabelle to meet his family. "My bride," he announced proudly. "Mrs. Annabelle Vasquez." His gaze was on her instead of his family, which is why he didn't miss the way she paled at his words.

"Pleased to meet you," she murmured politely. To her credit, there was only a hint of a tremor in her voice. She was putting on a brave front, which made Ethan inexplicably proud of her.

Happy tears streaked Paloma's face as he continued with the introductions. "This is—"

"His mother," she interrupted, holding out her arms to Annabelle. "In every way that matters, though I didn't give birth to him."

After a brief hesitation, Annabelle leaned in to accept her embrace.

"Which makes you my daughter-in-law," Paloma added, "in every way that matters."

A ghost of a smile lit Annabelle's pale features as she stepped back. "Thank you, ma'am."

"And these," Paloma babbled, waving at her other sons, "are mine, too. From the oldest to the youngest." She swiftly rattled off their names. "Jameson, Keegan, Carlton, Redding, Chevy, and Lance."

Ethan watched his bride in fascination as she shook hands with his brothers, summoning a gracious word for each one.

Paloma reached behind her to drag a lone cowboy from the front pew. "And this fellow is Garth Swingler. I believe the two of you have already met?" She gave Annabelle a curious look.

"Oh, yes!" Annabelle gushed. "He jumped from the stagecoach and guarded my back while I made a run for the church. I am very much in his debt."

He inclined his head at their huddle. "I'm an out-of-work range rider, so I wasn't in no hurry to be anywhere else."

Ethan gave him a sharp look. "Consider yourself hired." Offering him a job was the least he could do for looking after his bride-to-be. He hoped the fellow hadn't done it because he was sweet on her.

"Thank you, sir!" The dusty cowpoke looked ready to drop to his knees and kiss Ethan's boots.

Ethan couldn't help noticing the looks Jameson and Keegan were exchanging. They held overtones of both amazement and envy. Like him, the Fords had not expected a true lady to find her way to El Vaquero. He'd bested them all at the game of straws, and they knew it. He wouldn't be surprised if several more men in town threw their hats into the ring for a mail-order bride of their own before the day's end.

Jameson pulled Ethan aside while Annabelle was chatting with Paloma. "We have a team on patrol outside. I'm heading back out there now to make sure it's safe to escort our women home."

"I'm mighty grateful." Ethan didn't miss the way Jameson was already claiming Annabelle as one of theirs.

"Think nothing of it, brother. It's the least I could do in return for the way you took Gray's place today."

So, I'm not the only one who's noticed what's going on between him and your ma. "I have no regrets." Ethan was having difficulty tearing his gaze away from Annabelle.

"No, I think not." Jameson clapped him on the shoulders so hard that Ethan had to grit his teeth to keep from wincing. There were scratches and bruises covering every inch of him. Though the grizzly bear hadn't gotten his claws into Ethan's flesh, his body still ached as if it had been thoroughly mauled.

There was a flurry of activity inside the church, during which the Ford brothers rushed in and out of the building to monitor the bandit situation. Bo Stanley took the opportunity to have Ethan and Annabelle sign their wedding certificate along with The Western Moon Agency's contract. Annabelle, as it turned out, had already signed her section of the latter document. So had the attorney in Atlanta who'd worked in proxy for the owner of the mail-order bride agency — a Mr. P. Claiborne. Ethan had yet to meet the fellow. Jameson had provided Ethan with the initial application for a mail-order bride. Then he'd delivered it, along with Ethan's payment of the required fees, to the attorney.

Thus, Ethan became officially married on paper in addition to the vows he and Annabelle had exchanged in front of his friends.

Movement in the back of the church made him glance up from the paperwork. Jameson was poking his head through the door to give him the all clear signal.

Ethan crooked his arm at his bride. "May I escort you home?"

Giving him a nervous nod, she placed her fingers ever so

lightly on his arm, as if not quite certain she wanted to touch him.

Keegan met them at the base of the church steps with Ranger. "I found where you'd tethered him. It was very clever, hiding him in the canyons like you did."

Ethan nodded in satisfaction. He knew a thing or two about securing a horse.

"I'll ride him home if you want," Keegan offered. "You're more than welcome to hop into the wagon with Ma." He gestured toward the team of horses that were already hitched and ready to go. The Fords owned a fine rig with iron wheels and leather seats. It was one they'd specially ordered and shipped from Houston.

Ethan deliberated for a moment, giving his new wife a sideways glance. As hard as her life had been in recent days, there seemed little point in spoiling her beyond what he could normally provide. A wagon just so happened to be something he couldn't afford at the present.

"No, thank you. We'll ride my horse home. I'd be much obliged if you'd carry her bags in the wagon, though."

"It's your wedding day," Keegan protested in undertones, angling his head at Annabelle.

Ethan squared his shoulders, wishing they didn't ache so much. "I appreciate the offer, but I'll be providing for my own wife from now on."

"Very well." Keegan raised his hands defensively as he backed away. "No need to bite my head off."

Guilt stabbed Ethan at the thought he might have been too hasty with his decision. He bent his head closer to his bride. "In the event you missed that exchange, my brothers are offering you a ride up the mountain in their wagon. I don't yet own a rig of my own, so I'll be riding my horse. I reckon it should be your choice whether to ride with them or me." His sore bones didn't feel up to bumping around on a hard wagon seat, so he intended to remain in the comfort of his saddle regardless of what she chose to do.

For an answer, Annabelle stepped up to Ranger and patted his nose. "What's his name?"

Ethan's mouth froze on a stale cry of warning as Ranger dipped his long, dark head toward her. However, the horse merely leaned into her caress. He was a spirited stallion, not accustomed to being handled by anyone besides him and his brothers. Most folks who came near him got nipped for their efforts, including the Fords when they were teasing Ethan. His horse had an uncanny sense of loyalty.

Apparently, Annabelle was an exception to that rule. She spoke in sweet, soothing tones to Ranger. He nickered and preened in response.

"My word!" Ethan muttered to his bride. "I was afraid Ranger would just as soon bite you as—"

"Nonsense!" She stroked her delicate fingers down the horse's nose again. "This handsome fellow would never mistreat a lady, would you, boy?" She briefly pressed her cheek to the horse's neck. "It's good to meet you, Ranger. My name is Annabelle. I married your favorite fellow, so I hope you don't mind sharing him."

Pleased by his wife's choice to ride with him, Ethan stooped to cup his hands and offer her a leg up. She placed a narrow black boot in his palms and hopped effortlessly into the saddle, smoothing her skirts into place. Ethan leaped astride behind her and reached around her to hold the reins. "I apologize again for my filth and stench. I'll get cleaned up as soon as we reach the cabin."

She shoved her long blonde locks over her shoulder and gave him a mischievous look. "From the way the wind is blowing, you are downwind of me, sir, not the other way around. I dabbed on as much rosewater as I could before leaving the train, but I cannot vouch that it's covering all the dust from my travels."

He was unable to hold back a chuckle at her words. To him, she smelled like a slice of Heaven. "I've no complaints, ma'am." He resisted the urge to reach up and smooth back a few strands of hair that were blowing across her face. Though the two of them were well and truly wed, he didn't wish to rush his fences with her. He'd rather earn her trust first.

His righteous intentions, however, weren't taking into consideration the incline of the mountain path. It grew steeper, forcing his new bride to ride flush against him. At first, she tried to hold herself stiffly away from him. After a while, though, she relaxed in slow degrees. "I hope I'm not in your way," she murmured, when Ranger jostled them against each other as he sidestepped a rut in the road.

"Not at all, ma'am. I am yours to lean on whenever you wish." Warmth and wonder filled him at the way her delicate frame fit so perfectly against his.

"You are most kind." Her voice was bland. She tipped her head against his shoulder, giving up her fight against the steep incline. "I hope my weight isn't making your injuries any worse."

"Hardly." The genuine concern in her voice both surprised and entranced him. "You weigh no more than a firefly."

They were traveling in a loose formation, with Jameson up front and the wagon following behind them. The rest of the Ford brothers were staggered behind the wagon on the narrow path. Meanwhile, the range riders on patrol were fanning out across the mountain to ensure their safe passage onward and upward.

They arrived at Ethan's cabin first. It was perched on the rim of a plateau overlooking the mountain range. He'd purposefully built his home there for the view. The rest of his property stretched inward on a gradually decreasing slope that led down to an even bigger plateau where the rest of El Vaquero was located. Ford Ranch comprised the entire east side of town. The end of it butted up to Ethan's property.

He'd never tried to look at his log cabin through someone else's eyes, but he hoped his bride approved of her new home. Though he'd not planned to marry again this soon, he was grateful that the Fords had pushed him into building a four-room cabin with a second-story loft.

Jameson had teased him about being a big man and needing plenty of room for his brutish shoulders. In hindsight, however, Ethan now understood that he'd never intended for his top range rider to remain a bachelor.

"Is this your place?" Annabelle straightened in the saddle as they rode closer to his cabin. He immediately missed the warmth of her back pressed against his chest.

"No, it's *our* place," he corrected quietly. "Welcome home, Mrs. Vasquez."

She twisted her head to give him a tremulous smile. "You might as well use my given name now that we're married."

Awareness crackled between them. Her face was so close that all he would have to do was lean forward a few inches to steal the kiss she'd withheld from him earlier. He didn't, of course. He wouldn't attempt to kiss her again until she expressly indicated she wanted him to.

"Don't mind if I do, Annabelle." He liked the sound of her name rolling across his tongue. It was as soft and feminine as she was. He gave himself a mental shake and schooled his expression. It occurred to him that the way he was charmed by everything she said and did might be due to nothing more than how long he'd gone without a woman in his life.

"Mercy," she said beneath her breath as the path evened out, providing her first glimpse of his front porch.

His gaze narrowed on the porch, wondering what had

elicited such an exclamation. What did it mean? Was it good or bad? He scanned his home from the porch to the rooftop, trying to determine if something was wrong with it.

It was a simple home of logs with roughly hewn columns. Since she was from Atlanta, he supposed she was accustomed to bigger, fancier buildings. He kept a pile of firewood on the left side of the door and various farm tools propped against the wall on the right side. A spare saddle and a few saddle blankets were straddling the railing, hiding most of it from view. Come to think of it, it might not hurt to move them out to the barn now that he was wed.

He leaped to the ground, grimacing as the movement jarred his aching joints. Then he turned around to lift his bride down beside him.

"Go on in and make yourself at home. Keegan will have your bags unloaded from the wagon in no time. I'll join you after I get Ranger settled in the barn."

She nodded at him, wide-eyed, then silently glided up the porch steps to open the front door.

Her ensuing gasp twisted his heart. "Mercy!" she whispered again.

She sounded so scandalized that this time he was certain his home did not live up to her expectations. "Feel free to rearrange anything you want," he called over his shoulder as he led Ranger toward the barn. Disappointment clawed through his chest. He could only hope she would get used to the place in time.

Rearrange! Rearrange? Annabelle stood in the doorway of Ethan Vasquez's home, if a body could even call it that, wondering how any human could live in such a pig sty.

She could only presume the room she was standing in was

the living room. There was a sofa pushed against the wall that might have once been blue. It was difficult to tell since it was so threadbare and dusty. There were newspapers scattered on the floor around it.

There were no adornments on the walls, and the air smelled stale and overripe like dirty socks. She blinked at the sight of a hoe leaning against one corner of the room. *A hoe?* Who in the world kept a hoe in their living room?

A man cleared his throat behind her, making her whirl around.

"Ah...Keegan, is it?" she stammered.

"Yes, ma'am." It was difficult to see his eyes beneath the brim of his hat. He was gripping the handles of her travel bags. "Where would you like me to put these?"

She waved numbly at the porch, not yet sure if there was a clean square inch in the house for them.

He set them down with a gallant flourish beside the wood pile.

"Thank you."

"My pleasure. Give us a holler if you need anything else."

"Thank you," she said again.

She stared after him as he strode to the wagon. Paloma leaned over the side of it to wave at her.

She waved back and watched as they drove away. Then she gazed around the living room again, longing for her boarding house room. It was cramped sharing it with her closest friends, but they'd kept it tidy and clean, with a special emphasis on clean!

The only upside to the messy cabin she was standing inside was Ethan's blanket permission to let her move around anything she wanted.

As she took a quick tour of the place, she found herself hoping her husband wouldn't mind her moving a few things outside and a few other things into the garbage. The second room she entered was a kitchen. Other than a few dirty dishes on the cabinet top and in the sink, it was mostly bare — including the cupboards. Did the man not keep any food stocked? How did he survive? As she rounded the center preparation cabinet, she received another shock. A galvanized metal tub was resting directly in front of the fireplace — the kind of tub one bathed in.

Gulping a few times, she pushed open the door leading out back and found what she was looking for. About ten feet or so away from the porch rose the pump handle of a well. A scattering of buckets rested on the ground around it.

She pumped six of them full of water and carried them to the kitchen. Starting the fire, she hung them on hooks mounted inside the fireplace to warm. She made a few more trips, filling buckets and emptying them into the tub. In a matter of minutes, the water over the fire would be ready to add, warming it enough for a body to sit in.

The room adjoining the kitchen was utterly bare. After the clutter Annabelle had observed in the previous two rooms, it was a bit of a shock to find nothing but cobwebs and dust in this one. Movement near the toe of her left boot made her jump. It was a spider. She quickly brought the toe of her boot down on it. *Ick!* Now she would have to find something to clean it up with.

She had to return to the living room to reach the fourth and final room. As expected, it was a bedroom. It contained a bed that was unmade with trousers draped haphazardly across the footboard.

She wandered dazedly back into the living room, wondering where to even begin cleaning the place. On her way, she nearly bumped into a ladder built into the wall. Squinting upward, she perceived she was staring at a loft. *Egad!* It wouldn't exactly be easy or prudent to scale the crude ladder in a skirt.

Spinning around, she critically eyed the room and determined it was big enough to add a stairwell. *Ethan Vasquez, your home needs more than cleaning and rearranging.* It needed a few upgrades, too.

The clomping of boots on the porch steps alerted her to the fact that her husband was returning. She spun toward the door to greet him, halting him on the entry rug with an upraised hand.

He eyed her with concern. "Is everything alright?"

"No, but it will be shortly." Her voice was tight. "You said I could rearrange your home. May I clean it, as well?"

"Of course." A faint smile twisted his mouth. "It's your home now. Do as you wish."

"In that case, may we start by removing your boots at the door?"

He glanced down at them in puzzlement. "My boots? I usually leave them by the bed, so I can step right into them come morning."

"I would much prefer that you left them at the door." She pointed at the door mat, and added firmly, "Every time you enter the house, please."

Watching her curiously, he removed his boots and left them standing at the stated spot.

"Thank you. Now come." She waved him toward the kitchen. "I've drawn you a bath, and I imagine your wounds will need tending afterward."

"I don't require a nursemaid," he growled, though his footfalls followed her.

She ignored his crabbing, knowing it was merely a show of toughness. While growing up, she'd tended the various bumps, bruises, and cuts of her brothers. "One of your wounds looks like it might need stitches. Fortunately, I brought along plenty of needles and thread."

When he started to bluster, she waved him toward the fire.

"Your bath is nearly ready. I'll start setting the bed to rights while you clean up. You'd best fetch a change of clothing and a towel first." She held her breath, hoping he wouldn't expect her to tend to such matters while he bathed. It was too soon. They'd just met.

When he didn't answer, she exited the kitchen and waited on the other side of the door until she heard him pouring the warm buckets of water into the tub.

Then she moved silently to the bed to strip the soiled linens off.

Chapter 5: Upside-Down
ETHAN

Over the next week, Ethan's new wife scoured every inch of his cabin — from the loft to the cellar located beneath the pantry. He had no idea how she made it up to the loft on the blasted ladder he'd built into the wall. All he knew for sure was that the bedroll he'd tossed up there for himself remained clean and made up.

He tried being extra careful when he smoothed out the blankets each morning to save her the trouble of climbing up there. When he returned home after each long day on the range, though, the linens had been freshly fluffed and smoothed to perfection.

It was only one of many changes she made to his routine. He'd never taken so many baths in all his days. She made it clear that she expected them nightly.

"The other range riders will never stop poking fun at me as long as you keep me so clean," he muttered as he settled in a high-back cane chair for dinner. They were seated at a trestle table made of ash wood that didn't belong to him. No doubt Paloma was behind the gift, since Annabelle had made noises about dusting it off from some corner of the Fords' attic. In the past, he'd eaten standing. Or on his way out the door. Or in the saddle.

His bride trilled out a merry laugh, her cheeks as rosy as the frothy pink gown she wore as she bent her head for him to say grace. She'd stirred up a pot of beans for dinner and seasoned it with a few strips of his favorite dried meat.

"I've heard the rumors. Many of them wish to borrow me to come set their cabins to rights," she bragged in a merry voice. "I could easily hang a shingle and start charging for my services."

"No." His voice was sharp. The last thing he wanted was for his wife to become a drudge, working her fingers to the bone all over town.

Her smile slipped. "My back is strong." Her chin came up, making a few wispy blonde curls dance against her cheeks. "Let me earn my keep so I don't become a burden to you."

Though he was famished, he lowered his spoon to his bowl. "You are no burden, Annabelle. You do more than enough to earn your keep here. Everywhere you look is proof enough of that." He waved his hands to take in the room, hating how scarred his fingers were. During his temporary captivity one night on the range, they'd been deliberately held over a bonfire by bandits. "I honestly didn't know that a wood floor could be made to sparkle until you came along."

She frowned at him. "All the same, I'm running out of things to do, Ethan. The house is clean. Your shirts are mended." She half rose from her chair. "Other than redressing your wounds, that is."

"I am on the mend." He waved her back into her seat, wanting to enjoy a little more time with her before she flitted away.

She hesitated. "I almost forgot. Today is the day to remove your stitches."

"Later," he said firmly. "You should eat first."

She sat, pushing her spoon around her bowl without taking a bite. "I suppose I could try my hand at gardening." Her expression brightened with hope as she glanced up at him again.

"Have you ever planted a garden before?" On her mail-order bride application, she'd claimed to possess strong domestic skills, which she clearly excelled at. However, most of his outdoor chores had proven to be a mystery to her. He'd been required to demonstrate the simplest tasks, like milking a cow, which gave him no confidence in her ability to farm.

"No, but I cannot imagine it will be too difficult," she hastened to explain. "I used to watch my mother cultivate herb plants on the windowsill, and I know you own a hoe." This, she added with a grimace. "Pray recall that I recently relocated it from the living room to the barn."

He hadn't forgotten that or the many other things she'd relocated since her arrival. Very few items remained where he put them these days. He was forever having to hunt things down.

Trying to get a better grasp of the situation, he mused aloud, "How did you occupy your time back in Atlanta?"

His wife's expression grew resigned. "I took in laundry and mending, mostly."

"Before that," he corrected, regretting how much wind he'd inadvertently taken out of her sails. "When you were growing up, what did you do?"

Her long-suffering faded to a faraway look. "I sang." A sighing chuckle escaped her. "I played the pianoforte. I took dance lessons and attended parties. I painted watercolors. I took long walks through the gardens on our plantation. My friends and I would meet a few mornings per week to embroider linens, sometimes for wedding gifts and sometimes to add to a trousseau. They stayed for tea and luncheons afterward so we could gossip about all the handsome gentlemen in town — which of them we wanted to dance with and which of them we hoped to court. Then, one by one, they were called off to war." Her voice trembled. "Most of them never came back." She fell silent.

Ethan hardly knew what to say. Her words were a stark reminder of just how different they'd been raised. It was no wonder that her two travel bags had been stuffed with little more than gowns, stockings, sashes, and shoes. He'd married a southern belle. A high-society girl with upscale tastes. Under normal circumstances, she might have married one of the handsome young men she'd mentioned and lived out her days in comfort. Instead, she'd been saddled with a scarred cowboy who spent most of his time in the saddle instead of entertaining her. He earned enough money to keep a roof over her head and food in her belly, but that was about it.

While he studied her in troubled silence, she abruptly pushed back her chair and fled the room in a swirl of pink skirts.

He scraped back his own chair, intending to follow her. However, his stomach growled such a loud protest that he lifted his bowl and took a long, hearty slurp first. He knew it would scandalize his bride's sense of decorum to see him eat like an animal. However, she wasn't in the room to witness his lapse in manners.

He strode in his sock feet through the living room and found the front door cracked open. Annabelle was on the other side of it, leaning her elbows on the porch railing to gaze at the mountain peaks below.

He stooped his much taller frame to lean on the railing beside her, his heart clenching to note the wetness of tears on her cheeks.

She shot him a wry look. "I am sorry for being such a watering pot. My jaunt down memory lane is partly your fault, though."

He sorely wished he'd never brought up her past. "I beg your forgiveness for bringing up a topic that saddened you. I—"

"Oh, give way, Ethan!" She chuckled despite her tears. "I only meant you've been good to me."

Confusion swirled through his gut. He'd all but forgotten how difficult it was to follow the rapidly changing emotions of a woman. "And that makes you weep?"

"It means I have too much time on my hands to think about the past. Before I met you, I was working from sunup to sundown, then falling exhausted into bed. I was simply existing. Now that you've given me the chance to live again, I also have time to grieve again."

"I see." He understood the sentiment all too well since he'd spent the past several years trying to bury his own grief in much the same way — in one grueling hour of work after the other. He and his new wife had many differences, but this was something they had in common.

"For what it's worth, I like being cared for by you, too." He hadn't meant to speak so freely around her. However, her stint of soul-bearing seemed to have spurned a bit of it from him in return.

"Indeed?" She shot him an incredulous look, wiping her cheeks with the backs of her hands. "You seemed exasperated when I asked you to remove your boots by the door, and you've made it clear you don't want me fussing over your wounds."

"I was mostly surprised about your demands, but I've come to like them. I've come to like you." As he dipped his head closer to hers, he also liked the fact that she no longer shrank away from him like she had the day they'd met. He supposed he could credit all the baths she'd made him take for that bit of progress, since he no longer offended her nose. Plus, the fact that he'd shaved his face smooth and trimmed his hair

for her. She hadn't asked him to, but it seemed prudent to clean up his appearance since she was cleaning up everything else around him.

She caught her lower lip between her teeth at his perusal, though she didn't deliver a response to his confession that he'd come to like her. *Pity*. He was curious to hear what she thought about him in return.

"I expected there would be a few changes in my life when I wed," he drawled, waggling his eyebrows at her in the hope it would drag a smile from her.

She wrinkled her nose at him. "What did you really want in a wife, Ethan? I can all but guarantee you weren't looking to take on an impoverished southern miss, certainly not one with a knack for attracting bandits."

It was true. He hadn't expected her — her stunning beauty, the way she'd turned his cabin into a real home, or the trouble she'd brought with her. He and the Fords had been forced to add his cabin and property to their regular patrols. Not a day went by that they didn't send a bandit or two running back down the mountain. It was probably one of the reasons his bride was feeling so cooped up. For safety reasons, she hadn't been able to stray too far from home yet.

Knowing it wasn't wise to confide in his wife about the game of straws, he settled for a neutral answer. "You confessed to being bored." He appreciated her honesty and was determined to do whatever he could to relieve her boredom in the coming days. "So, I'll confess to something as well. I've been lonely. I enjoy my work, but I was tired of coming home to an empty house every night." It was true. After the death of his first wife, his home had become achingly silent.

"Even though marrying me meant cleaning up your act a little?" Annabelle's voice was teasing.

"A little?" He straightened to stare at her in astonishment.

"Woman, you have turned my entire life upside-down with all of your fussing, tending, and incessant cleaning."

She straightened her spine and lifted her chin. "Who else do I have to fuss over?"

Tension crackled between them at her admission that he was the center of her attention, whether either of them liked it or not. It made him feel all the more guilty about how much time he had to spend apart from her. It also made him long to restore some of the luxuries she'd been accustomed to in the past — things like music and painting to help her days pass more pleasantly.

Her lips parted to say something else, and Ethan's gaze dropped to her mouth. Her lips were pink and full. At the moment, they were twisted into a faint pout. Ever since the moment they'd wed, he'd been daydreaming about sampling them. Soon, he hoped.

Swallowing the temptation, he angled his head at the door. "How about we finish our dinner? Then I'll let you fuss all you want over my scratches and bumps."

Annabelle sucked in a breath at his words, frowning at him. "You do realize you were nearly mauled by a bear."

He spread his hands, utterly enchanted by her vehemence on his behalf. "I was present, so I remember every detail."

"You need to be more careful." In a swirl of pink skirts, she sailed past him into the cabin.

He followed behind her, mulling over his response as he locked the new bolt he'd installed after her arrival. "I do not go looking for trouble. It comes looking for me, or rather the cattle." His sudden urge to defend himself was an odd feeling. He'd simply been doing his job. How could she not see that?

When they reached the kitchen, he stood until she took a seat. Then he rejoined her at the table and hungrily lifted his spoon. Between bites, he explained, "Predators are always on the lookout for a sick cow. Or one that strays too far from the herd. Or even a newborn, which was the case on our wedding day."

"Oh-h-h-h!" Annabelle gave a mournful sigh, lowering the bite of soup she was about to place in her mouth. "Pray assure me you saved the calf."

"I did. That's why I looked so wretched by the time I met you at the church. The bear refused to mosey on after suitable encouragement." The encounter had quickly turned hostile.

"You shot him, didn't you?" She looked both horrified and fascinated.

"He left me no choice. It is my job to protect the herds."

She thoughtfully pursed her lips. "Even so, I meant what I said about you being more careful."

"I am careful, Annabelle. I would not lie to you about something so important." Though his job was dangerous at times, he wasn't a thrill seeker and avoided taking unnecessary risks.

"Please be more careful, anyway," she insisted firmly.

"Why?" He didn't think it was possible to be any more vigilant than he already was.

"Because I know about the extra patrols around our home, and I've seen the new bolts you installed on the front and back doors." She shifted in her seat. "Which means you are the only thing standing between me and *my* predators. Though we barely know each other, I am depending on you now."

He'd not pressed her for any more information about the bandits beyond what she'd told him on their wedding day. However, her words made him wonder again if she knew more than what she was telling him. "No one will get to you, Annabelle, without going through me. That I can assure you."

"Thank you." An amicable silence settled between them as they finished their beans.

He finally scooted back his chair and rolled up his sleeves. "I am fed and ready to be fussed over."

Looking amused, Annabelle stood and started to collect their bowls and spoons.

He reached for them. "It's my turn to wash them."

"I don't mind the task." She didn't release her grip on them. "I have precious little to do as it is."

His fingers slid over hers. "Be that as it may, I cannot have you slaving over me day and night." He gave the dishes a gentle tug to release them from her grasp. "Who do you think washed the dishes before we were wed?"

"No one, I reckon." She relinquished the bowls to him at last. "They were scattered all over the kitchen cabinets when I arrived."

His jaw dropped at her sass.

"Oh, wait!" she chortled. "The dishes weren't merely scattered throughout the kitchen. I seem to recall a mug on the floor in the living room, too, and another one on your nightstand."

"Why, you little minx!" He set down the bowls and made a swipe for her.

She danced out of his reach, chuckling as she left the room.

He stared after her, thoroughly entertained by the way she was forever picking and poking at him. No one had ever treated him like this before. The fact that she seemed to enjoy teasing him gave him hope for their marriage — that she would someday find him worthy of her affections. Because she was fast worming her way into his.

She returned to the kitchen with her sewing basket.

He was still washing dishes in the basin beneath the window overlooking their back yard. She silently joined him, setting down her sewing kit on the cabinet and reaching for a towel.

He pulled a second towel off the shelf beneath the basin, and they dried the two bowls and spoons in companionable silence. Neither of them spoke until the dishes were returned to the overhead shelf. He felt her eyes on him, though.

"Fussing time," she announced shyly, reaching for her sewing basket. She pointed at the chair he'd vacated at the table.

He obediently sat, holding his arms akimbo so she could get a better look at them.

"They're better." She gently palpated the skin above and below the abrasions on each arm. "Pray forgive me, but I'm afraid this next part is going to be uncomfortable."

He rolled his eyes. "Do your worst, woman. I can handle it." He didn't even flinch when she began removing the stitches. He was too busy enjoying her soft touch.

"I know it stings." She made a clucking sound of sympathy. "I have a salve that I can apply afterward to soothe it."

"Or," he waited until she lifted her small scissors from his bicep to finish his sentence, "you are more than welcome to distract me from my suffering with a kiss." He'd not intended to make any more romantic overtures until he was sure she was ready. However, being this close to her was doing crazy things to his head.

"Ethan!" She dropped her scissors. They clattered to the floor beside his chair.

"Did you or did you not just state that you wished to soothe the pain in my arm?" he demanded playfully.

"I did, but—"

"This will do the trick better than anything else."

She stared down at him, her cheeks blooming like roses. "You're quite serious?"

"That I am, wife." He felt his lids grow heavy beneath her shy perusal. "Trust me. It will work."

"Very well, then." Blushing wildly, she bent her head over his forehead.

Not that. The longing for a real kiss from his bride was too great. Ethan snaked an arm around her waist and tumbled her into his lap.

She grasped his shoulders, staring wide-eyed in astonishment at him. "Oh!" The breath whooshed out of her. "You want...that."

"Yes, Annabelle. Very much." He held her gaze, allowing her to see the longing in his eyes. "May I kiss you?"

"I...yes." She swayed closer, looking dizzy.

He palmed the back of her neck to draw her gently forward. Then he brushed his lips over hers. They were as soft as he'd imagined they would be, as sweet and giving as the rest of her.

His heart pounded from the heady rush that followed. Annabelle Vasquez was beautiful on the inside and out, and she was his. He'd not expected to feel this way again about any woman. Sure, he figured they'd eventually rear a family together, which would require a certain level of intimacy, but what he was feeling for her was more than that.

As he poured his heart into their kiss, he recognized the fact that she was stirring his emotions in ways that hadn't been in the fine writing of their contract. It was real. It was special. It was good.

He hoped she was feeling at least a small part of what he was feeling.

ANNABELLE HAD NEVER KISSED A MAN BEFORE. SHE'D wanted to. She'd daydreamed about it. Once, she'd almost been kissed at a dance. Her handsome partner had escorted her to a balcony outside, where the moon and stars could work their magic on their young sensibilities. Alas, her father had found them there and put an end to the magic before it could blossom into more.

None of the kisses she'd imagined, however, could hold a candle to the way her husband was kissing her now. His mouth was gentle and caressing, yet firm and possessive. The way he was making her feel was confusing — like laughing and crying at the same time. Even more puzzling, it left her wanting more.

He raised his head with an exhale that she couldn't quite define. Was it the same longing she was feeling or something else?

"That, my dear wife, is how you make a man forget everything else."

"Everything?" she whispered.

"Everything," he returned, tracing the curve of her chin with his scarred thumb, "except you."

She scanned his rugged features, trying to figure out what it was about him that stirred her so. Despite the tender moment they were sharing, she knew he wasn't a man to be crossed. She'd seen him in action. With a weapon in hand, he was a very dangerous creature, indeed. *Good gracious!* Without a weapon in hand, he still was. He was big, strong, and clever. One bear, in particular, and a whole pile of bandits were already regretting locking horns with him.

"Allow me to ask you one more thing." He cupped her face in his hands, banked emotions steeping in his gaze.

"What is it?" She gazed back, caught up in the warmth and wonder she read there. She wished she was bold enough to touch his face, to slide her fingertips over the evening shadow darkening his strong jaw.

"Are you satisfied with your end of our bargain? The marrying me part?"

"I am." She knew he was referring to their mail-order contract now that they'd met and had the opportunity to get to know each other a little better. Inevitably, it reminded her of the plight of her friends back in Atlanta. However, it didn't feel like the right moment to tell him how many other impoverished southern belles were just as anxious to wed as she had been. It was a topic she intended to bring up with him soon, though.

"I'm glad to hear it." Without any further ado, he stood with her and allowed her limbs to slide slowly to the ground. "I'd like to keep you happy with your end of the bargain, so we'd best circle back to the topic of how you may fill your time while I'm away."

He reached for her hand and tucked it into the crook of his arm. "Come out back with me. There's something I want to show you."

She felt a twinge of remorse at the fact he had to unbolt the door to let them outside. Until her arrival, he'd lived without any locks on his doors.

He led her to the side of the barn closest to the mountain drop-off. "If you're serious about planting a garden for us, it only makes sense to place it near the barn. That way you'll be near the well water, farm tools, and fertilizer." The last item he added with a smirk.

"I am serious about it, Ethan." She stepped away from him to take a closer look at the plot of ground he'd chosen. It was actually a series of plots — areas he or someone else had leveled off to form tiers against the side of the mountain.

"Did you do all of this?"

He grimaced. "I know it isn't much. I've barely gotten started."

"It's perfect." She could already imagine the mountainside blossoming with sprouts and green things, just like her ma's windowsill had.

"There are seeds and gardening tools in the barn, and I am happy to counsel you in the basics of planting," his voice held a note of caution, "but I will not be here to tend the plots with you or help you guard them against marauders."

"I will remain vigilant," she assured firmly. "I need something to do besides clean your home." Something that would make her feel like she was making a bigger contribution. She didn't want to do most of the taking in their marriage, while he did most of the giving.

"It's your home, too," he reminded. "Heaven knows it didn't gleam like diamonds before you showed up."

Though she knew he was trying to be funny, she didn't smile. "I really do need to stay busy. It's the only thing that's kept me sane in recent months." That, and her ceaseless praying for wisdom, comfort, and strength as she slowly pieced herself back together after the war.

He eyed her curiously. "If I may be so bold, is there someone else you're missing besides the family you lost?"

"It is kind of you to ask." She twirled back in his direction. "Yes. I left some very dear friends behind. They made me promise to write them as soon as I could to let them know I made it safely to Texas."

"Friends," he repeated. It sounded more like a question than a statement.

She drew a deep breath. Maybe it was the right time, after all, to confide in him about Penelope and the others. "There's something you should probably know about me," she said slowly.

"Oh?" His expression grew shuttered as he waited.

"My friends are the only reason I survived as long as I did after the war. We grew up together and suffered the same fate together. After losing our families and homes, we reunited on a city street one afternoon and came up with a plan to survive. For the past year, we've shared a room in a boarding house and every penny that we made. We took in laundry and mending, anything we could do to keep food in our bellies."

His expression cleared. "So, these friends of yours are women? All of them?"

"Yes."

He looked so relieved that she perceived he'd been worried about a potential attachment to a gentleman back home. It gave her the courage to continue. "When we ran across an advert for The Western Moon Agency, it felt like the answer to our prayers. An opportunity to start fresh and build a better life somewhere else. Because of my acute financial troubles, I insisted on going first."

For reasons she didn't understand, his dark eyes started to twinkle. "Exactly how many friends did my lovely bride leave behind?"

"Five. Not only are they anxious to hear of my safe arrival, they are waiting for me to advise them whether it is safe to follow in my footsteps."

"To become a mail-order bride?"

"Yes."

"And what do you intend to tell them in your letter?"

"It's already written, and I've assured them they would be better off taking their chances out west as opposed to remaining in Atlanta."

"Despite the bandits, eh?" His dark eyes twinkled.

"Yes. If I give you the letter, will you ensure that it gets mailed?"

"You know I will." There was both tenderness and empathy in his voice, plus a hint of triumph that she didn't understand.

She briefly closed her eyes to summon the courage to broach the toughest part of what she needed to say. "You don't, by any chance, know of any other range riders interested in wedding impoverished southern ladies?" He didn't owe her any favors, but her friends had been loyal to her. They deserved no less than her loyalty in return.

"I just might." He grinned. "Let me talk with a few of the other fellows and see what they say."

"Thank you." Tears of relief stung the backs of her eyelids. *There.* She'd done what she could. Now came the waiting and the praying. "I'll get started on our garden in the morning." Swallowing the flood of emotions at the thought of seeing her friends again, she turned toward the barn. "I reckon I should bring the farm tools down from the loft."

"The loft?" He sounded shocked.

"Yes. I stored the hoe up there yesterday that you used to have in your living room, along with a shovel and a rake."

His jaw tightened. "I'll get them down for you. It's not safe up there."

She frowned in surprise. "I thought it was a new barn." It certainly looked new.

"It is, but I'm still working on parts of it. I'd prefer that you stay out of the loft for now." His expression indicated that the subject was closed.

"Very well." Irritation flared in her gut. So much for his home being her home, too! It made her wonder if he had something to hide up in the loft.

The awareness that had been zinging between them after dinner faded.

"I reckon we ought to turn in now." Ethan's voice was polite but distant. "The morning will be here before we know it."

Annabelle grimaced, knowing he meant he would leave before daybreak and be gone again until dinner time. She could only hope the gardening project would be enough to fill the hours he was away. "I'll leave my letter on the kitchen table."

He nodded. "I'll take it with me to the ranch and have one of the Fords carry it to the post office in El Gato on their next trip."

"Thank you, Ethan." She was truly grateful for his willingness to do what he could to help her friends.

"My pleasure, Annabelle." A caressing note crept back into his voice as he crooked his arm at her.

As she took his arm, the awareness between them intensified again. However, he bid her adieu at the door of their bedroom, making no attempt to kiss her again.

Disappointment filled her as she stepped inside the room alone.

Chapter 6: Alarming Discoveries
ANNABELLE

One month later

Annabelle woke to the sound of her husband climbing down the ladder from his second-story sleeping loft. For the past several weeks, she'd listened to his footsteps as he made his way through the house, preparing for another long, hard day of work. It filled her with a restless energy she couldn't explain.

Though it was still dark, she decided to give in to the restless energy and make an appearance. Sitting up in bed, she rummaged around the linens for the robe she'd tossed off in the middle of the night. Tugging it around her shoulders, she slid her feet over the side of the bed and stepped into her slippers. She made her way to the basin and washed her face. Then she padded into the living room, holding a candle in front of her.

Ethan was by the front door, tugging on his boots. "Annabelle!" He paused to eye her in concern. "Is everything alright?" His large frame was angled in her direction, poised to take action.

"Yes, of course. I heard you moving around the house, is

all." She drank in the sight of his impressive height and broad shoulders. Despite the plain, faded shirt and denim trousers he wore, he was a striking man. Not handsome, in the traditional sense. Handsome was too tame a word for such arresting features. She was fast coming to adore the way his dark eyes always lit at the sight of her. It never failed to make her feel special — like she mattered to him. It was a good feeling, one she looked forward to feeling again and again and again.

She liked the way he moved, too. A man who made his livelihood patrolling the herds, his sinewy limbs contained the suppressed energy of a mountain lion ready to pounce. He was ever vigilant, ever watchful. Right now, he was watching her with an intensity that made her shiver.

"I'm sorry I woke you." His voice was husky from having so recently shrugged off the webs of slumber.

"I'm a light sleeper. I hear you leave for work every morning." She knew she was staring, but she found it difficult to tear her gaze away from him. His bronze skin brought to mind the statues of Roman warriors. She'd seen pictures of them inside the books in her family's library while growing up.

"Even so, there is no need for you to rise at such an early hour." He finished stepping into his boots.

She smiled faintly. "Who else is there to bid you goodbye?"

His lips twitched. "No one but the crickets."

"Until now," she reminded, setting the candle tray on the mantle and gliding closer to him.

Something flared in his dark gaze. She wasn't sure who moved first, only that they ended up in each other's embrace.

"I shall miss you while you're away," she confessed, burying her face against his chest.

A silent chuckle rumbled through him as his hands tangled in her hair. "This wasn't supposed to happen." He spoke the words to himself. She wasn't sure if she was intended to hear them.

"What wasn't supposed to happen?" Her voice was muffled against the cotton fabric of his shirt.

"You, I reckon." He rested his cheek against the top of her head. "The whole mail-order bride situation was Jameson Ford's idea. It was part of his plan to settle the town. Like you, I volunteered to go first. I never dreamt I would wed a woman so lovely. One who would turn my sparse cabin into a real home and make me anxious to return to her every evening."

"Ethan!" She flushed at his words, tipping her head back to gaze up at him. "Do you really look forward to coming home to me?"

"Every minute of every day." He smoothed one large hand over her hair, watching her from beneath heavy lids.

Her insides melted at the glint of approval she read there. There was admiration, too. And pride. She playfully gripped his shirt to mask the answering stir of emotions inside her. "Here and I was half afraid you dreaded coming home on account of the baths."

"Hardly." His voice was teasing as he reached up to cover her hands with his. "Whatever it takes to please my wife."

She was grateful for the shadows to hide the blush that was spreading all the way to her toes. "It would please your wife even more," she informed him softly, "to kiss her husband goodbye."

His chest rose and fell rapidly. There was a pregnant pause, in which she feared he was going to deny her request.

Then his hands tightened over hers. "Well, the last thing I would want to do is displease you, darlin'."

Her heart thrilled at his use of the endearment. He'd never called her that before. Before she could catch her breath, he swooped in to seal his mouth over hers.

It was as if the sun rose ahead of the dawn. Every fiber in her body lit with happiness as he cherished her with his lips and hands. He didn't stop with one kiss or two, plundering her mouth repeatedly with a hunger that shook her.

They were both breathing unevenly by the time he lifted his head. "I have to go." His callused thumb dragged across the underside of her chin.

"Do you?" Her voice was soft and beseeching.

"I wish I didn't." He dragged his fingers lightly across her cheek. "I'm sorry I have to leave you alone so much. How about I invite Paloma Ford to pay you a visit this afternoon?"

She chuckled and gently swatted away his hand. "I don't need a nursemaid any more than you do. Paloma is busy enough, delivering new babes all over the countryside."

His gaze inexplicably darkened at her words, but she plowed onward. "That said, she's invited us to lunch on Sunday after church. She and I can visit then."

His hand lingered on her cheek. "Are you sure there's no other reason I need to worry about you? I'm not accustomed to seeing you rise before I depart."

She could understand his confusion. It was the first time she'd done it the entire month they'd been married. "You'll get used to it." She flipped a hank of hair over her shoulder, reveling in the way his gaze followed her every movement. "I'm still learning how to be a wife, and I will no doubt make many mistakes along the way. However, rising to bid you goodbye this morning feels right."

"It does." He gave her cheek one last caress before dropping his hand. "May the hours fly, so I can return to you all the sooner."

"Then I'll say goodbye, so the hours can take wing."

As he reluctantly made his exit, she vowed to rise even sooner tomorrow so she could make him breakfast. They didn't get much time together, so she was going to have to make each snippet of time count, no matter how small.

She was aware of the strips of dried meat he carried in his

saddle bag, but a proper wife could easily send him off with something more filling. Lance Ford had dropped off a dozen eggs yesterday and some of the bear meat he and his brothers had cured from Ethan's kill. Though she'd never cooked bear meat before, it couldn't be much different from cooking other meats.

Smiling, she returned to their bedroom, humming to herself. Though it was still dark outside, she was no longer sleepy, so there was no point in climbing back between the sheets. She continued to hum as she made the bed. Then she removed her robe and padded barefoot in her chemise to the ladder leading to the loft. Nimbly scaling it, she moved across the room to smooth her husband's bedroll.

Though it was gallant of him to give her the use of the only bedroom in the house, it made her heart constrict at the thought of him sleeping like this indefinitely on the hard wooden floor. She'd not expected him to remain up here alone this long. As the weeks ticked past, it troubled her more and more.

So many days had passed since their first kiss, that she'd begun to worry she'd displeased him somehow. She'd feared that he was disappointed in marrying a southern miss more versed in the art of dancing and singing than living off the land. However, his kisses this morning had assured her that his interest in her was still very much intact.

What, then, was holding him back from making her entirely his? According to her mail-order bride contract, their marriage was still in its trial period. If they did not consummate it soon, their union could be annulled.

She shivered at the thought of being back at the mercy of unconscionable men like Dale Allard Featherfall.

"I won't go back," she announced fiercely to the empty loft. Though she'd started off unfit for pioneer living, she was quickly learning. After only a few weeks in the mountains, she could now milk a cow, saddle a horse, scavenge for wild berries and roots, and was trying her hand at gardening.

Her friends would be amazed to see how much she'd changed when they finally laid eyes on her again. As for her part, she was starved for news about them and couldn't wait until they wrote her back. Due to El Vaquero's remote location, Ethan had warned it could take months for any letters to reach them.

Before fluffing his pillow, she bent to press her cheek to it, breathing in his manly scent. Thanks to her, it was clean and soapy these days, which gave her an idea. Slipping back down the ladder, she lifted her bottle of rosewater from the dresser and dabbed it on her neck and wrists. Then she returned to her husband's bedroll in the loft. Lifting his pillow, she hugged it tightly, resting her cheek against it again.

There. Setting it back in place, she tentatively sniffed the air. The next time he settled down to sleep, his bed linens would bear her scent. If he was waiting for an invitation to return to his bedroom, hopefully he would realize she was extending one.

Blushing at her brazenness, she made her way back to the bedroom to dress for the day. The blue dress she'd worn during the first part of her journey west had become the dress in which she completed her daily chores. It would suit just as well for gardening.

As she buttoned her bodice, her gaze landed on her father's gold watch she kept displayed next to her brush and comb. Picking it up, she turned it over to read the inscription on the back: *Remember the good times.*

She smiled, finding comfort in the words. It was just like her father to have something like that engraved on his watch. He'd been a visionary, a man bursting with hopes and dreams for a future he'd never gotten to see due to the war. He'd understood that the agricultural industry in the south was waning in comparison to the more industrialized north. In an effort to compete, he'd taken out a mortgage on their home to invest in a railroad spur. It was way too bad she would never get to know what had become of it. If he'd lived, she had no doubt he would've recouped his investment and then some.

But there was no point in dwelling on *if's*. Sighing, Annabelle flicked at the lid of the watch with her thumbnail, trying to open it. As usual, she wasn't successful. It had been jammed shut the entire time it was in her possession. *Ah, well.* She returned it to its place on the dresser. Someday, she would take it to a jeweler to have it repaired. Not that it really mattered. It always soothed her sadness just to see it resting there every time she entered the room.

The hoot of an owl in the distance had her spinning toward the open window. It was time to button up the hatches for the day before it became too hot. As she moved toward the window, a second owl hoot gave her pause.

Unless her ears were deceiving her, it was different from the first one. The two owls continued to hoot as she stood by the window, almost as if they were communicating with each other.

Communicating! Oh, good heavens! That's exactly what they were doing, because they weren't owls at all. They were men. Not the Ford brothers and their regular patrols, though. She was familiar with their calls to each other, and they didn't hoot like owls — certainly not like owls who were right now making their way closer to the cabin.

Panic spurted through her midsection. For all she knew, the bandits were returning to take another shot at her. Where, oh, where was the patrol that normally kept watch on this side of the mountain? Her heart raced in trepidation as she spun in a full circle, searching for a place to hide.

The bed sat too high. Anyone who entered the room would easily spot her. The cellar was another possibility, but there was no place to hide down there if it was breached. The walls were lined with shelves, but there were no cupboards to climb inside or benches to crawl under.

Help me, Lord! More panic spurted as the hooting grew closer. They were coming from the road outside the cabin, which meant the rear door was her best chance of escape.

Wishing she had time to don her hat and shoes, she doused the candle on her nightstand. Snatching up her father's watch, along with the pistol she kept on a hook behind the nightstand, she tiptoed from the bedroom to the kitchen. Easing the back door open, she let herself out and shut it noiselessly behind her. She crept down the steps and made her way to the barn.

With trembling hands, she saddled Spots and prepared to mount her. The sound of shattering wood made her flinch. *Mercy!* As best as she could figure, someone had breached the front door of the cabin.

Leading the prancing Mustang to the back of the barn, Annabelle moved in front of her to slide open the barn door. "Don't worry," she crooned softly. "We're leaving." She hated leaving the cow behind, but it couldn't be helped.

A second crash sounded as the back door of the cabin was kicked from its hinges. She could hear it clatter across the porch planks.

Spots shrieked in alarm and reared back on her hind legs, cycling her hooves in the air. Annabelle had to leap aside to avoid being pummeled. The moment the horse came back down on all fours, she bolted from the barn.

Shouts sounded outside the barn. "There she is!" one man howled.

"I'll go after her," a second man shouted. "You stay and search the place." Soon, she could hear horses' hooves pounding after the frightened Mustang.

Trembling in fear, Annabelle pressed her body against the

wall, where her shoulder blades came in contact with one of the ladders leading to the loft. Instead of taking the stairs to the main part of the loft where Ethan stored his hay, sometimes he climbed the ladders he'd built into the walls on either side of the barn.

She'd only been up on this end of the loft once when she was looking for a place to stow the hoe and rakes. It was then that she'd spotted a scattering of storage chests and other odds and ends covered by cloths. She'd not gone back up there to explore what was in them after Ethan's warning that it wasn't safe to do so. Upon reflection, however, there were plenty of things to hide behind up there.

Swiftly tucking her skirts into her sash, she moved as silently as she could up the ladder. More crashes rent the air from inside the cabin. It sounded like whoever was searching the place was destroying it one piece at a time. Windows were shattered, and dishes were tossed onto the porch.

Tears of terror leaked down Annabelle's cheeks as she reached the loft and climbed through the square hatch. Crouching against the floor, she found it just as she remembered it. The shadowy outline of trunks rose on both sides of her. Since the intruder was making so much noise next door, she figured she had a minute or two to search for a decent hiding place.

She hastily flung open the lid to the first trunk. To her amazement, there was a dress inside. A woman's dress, not that of a small child. Beneath it was an enormous Bible and a set of delicately embroidered bed linens.

Egad! Annabelle silently lowered the lid, wondering who they'd belonged to. His mother, perhaps? Ethan had briefly mentioned his parents' passing, but it sounded like something that had happened a long time ago. The dress Annabelle had discovered looked newer, no more than a few years old.

The second trunk was filled with baby items — a toy

horse, a silver cup and spoon, a stack of cloth diapers, and a tiny quilt embroidered with horses.

The sound of stomping alerted her to the fact that the intruder was making his way down the back porch steps. She was out of time. Scanning the remaining trunks, her gaze settled on an oblong item covered in burlap. It was positioned in the corner of the room behind another pair of trunks.

Tiptoeing across the loft, she lifted the flap of burlap covering it and climbed beneath it. Her knees pressed into a patch of straw while her hands traveled over the wooden item. It was shaped like a large rectangular box, open at the top, a box which moved on its legs as she leaned against it.

And then she knew.

It was a baby cradle. This must be the reason her husband hadn't wanted her in the loft. He didn't want her to see the mementoes he was storing that had belonged to some other woman and child from his past. Probably not a sister or friend, because there would be no reason to keep such things hidden from his new wife. The only logical explanation was that Ethan Vasquez had been married before.

Her heart quaked at the memory of his words from this morning.

"This wasn't supposed to happen."
"What wasn't supposed to happen?"
"You, I reckon."

He'd gone on to say that the mail-order bride contract he'd signed had been Jameson Ford's idea — part of the plan to settle the town of El Vaquero. She pressed a hand to her middle at the realization he'd been trying to tell her that marrying again hadn't been his idea. He'd been pressured by his friends to do it, which could only mean one thing. He was still in love with the woman whose dress lay in the trunk a few feet away. That was the real reason he chose to sleep alone upstairs, night after night.

It felt like a fist was closing around her heart, squeezing it until she could hardly breathe through the pain.

The footfalls of the intruder grew closer, reclaiming her attention. She removed her pistol from the pocket of her dress and grasped it with fingers that shook. This would be her final stand. The outcome of it almost didn't matter any longer.

Fleeing west had been a mistake, since her enemies had so easily been able to track her here. Marrying Ethan had apparently been another mistake. She'd pledged her life to a man who had no desire to start a family with her, because his heart was already taken.

There were more slamming sounds as the outlaw pilfered through Ethan's riding gear. The longhorn mooed in alarm.

"Where did she hide the stolen goods, you filthy beast?" The angry question elicited yet more moos from the pitiful creature.

Stolen goods? Annabelle's eyelashes fluttered against her cheeks. What stolen goods? She'd not stolen anything. All she owned was the dress on her back and a handful of other belongings. Who in tarnation would make such a claim?

Mr. Featherfall's name flitted across her mind. *But of course.* He must be behind this, but why? Why, in heaven's name, would he claim she was a thief? What did he want from her?

"Don't see why he doesn't have the chit arrested for stealing and be done with it." The man kicked the stairs leading up to the loft, making the cow bawl in fear.

A shot was fired. Then another.

"Let's get out of here!" a man shouted from outside the barn. Annabelle could only presume that the first robber had returned. Moments later, the pounding of hooves could be heard as the intruders made their getaway.

"Annabelle!" Ethan's bellow reverberated through the cabin.

The sound of her husband's voice made her slump to the floor of the loft in relief, too frozen from what had just occurred to immediately call back to him. She listened numbly to the increasing level of urgency in his voice as he called her name until he was hoarse. Though she knew it was foolish of her to read anything into it, she took heart in the frantic sound of his voice.

More men arrived. Annabelle heard Jameson declare worriedly, "We found Spots with her saddle still on. Annabelle must have tried to get away."

"Do you think they have her?" Ethan's voice was so bleak that a silent sob escaped her.

"There's no telling." Their voices grew closer as they returned the horse to the barn. Her frightened whinnies tore at Annabelle's heart.

"I want every inch of this mountain searched." Ethan's voice was cold. "Every man we can spare. Patrols around the clock until..." His voice broke.

"We're going to find her, brother."

"Don't make any promises you can't keep. Let's just...get to work."

Annabelle's pistol slid from her nerveless fingers and clattered to the floor of the loft. "Ethan," she whimpered.

The barn grew strangely silent. "Did you hear that?" Jameson cried sharply.

"Ethan," Annabelle sobbed in a stronger voice. "Up here. I'm up here."

"It's her!" her husband shouted joyfully.

She could hear him scrambling up the ladder. Then there was a scraping sound as he shoved aside one of the chests. He opened and closed a few others.

"Over here," she called, finally summoning the strength to push aside the burlap.

His hands closed around her upper arms, lifting her from her hiding place. "Annabelle," he crooned over and over again as his large hands moved up and down her arms and across her shoulders. "What did they do to you? Where are you hurt?"

"I am fine," she assured shakily. At least, physically. Her heart felt like it was shattered into thousands of pieces behind her ribcage.

"You're bleeding," he accused, lifting one of her wrists for a closer look.

"It's nothing. I can barely feel it."

"Tell me what happened," he demanded as he gathered her in his arms and cuddled her against his chest.

She was tempted to burrow closer, but she held back, reminding herself that his heart belonged to someone else. "I, ah...there were owls hooting," she intoned stiffly. "They didn't sound right, so I grabbed my pistol and headed for the barn. I saddled Spots, but she got spooked and took off without me. Two men on horses arrived and started kicking down doors, so I hid up here."

"I thank the good Lord that you did." His voice was tight with emotion as he hoisted her in his arms and carried her down the stairs leading from the hayloft.

Keegan met them at the bottom, white-faced with worry. "Is she—?"

"I'm fine," Annabelle murmured, but she was unable to keep her voice from trembling.

"She's in shock," Ethan said flatly. "I fear she's worse off than she's letting on."

"I'll take her to my mother. She'll know what to do."

"Yes, please. I don't want her seeing the cabin before I can get it cleaned up." To Annabelle's alarm, Ethan deposited her in Keegan's arms. "Don't let her out of your sight before I return."

"Count on it, brother." There was a sigh in Keegan's voice as he added, "And where might you be going?"

"To pay a long overdue visit to the sheriff in El Gato. Then I'm going to hire the best lawyer I can afford. Over my dead body is some two-bit crook from Atlanta going to continue terrorizing my wife for the rest of her days."

Tears dripped down Annabelle's cheeks at the fury behind his words. Perhaps a part of him had come to care for her, after all. It wasn't enough, though. It would never be enough.

Oh, how the truth hurt! But she might as well face it. She'd been competing with a ghost for her husband's attentions since the moment they'd wed.

Chapter 7: Guest Room Getaway
ETHAN

Ethan kept an eye out for bandits the entire ride to El Gato. Jameson had insisted on accompanying him and bringing along a trio of their most trusted range riders to watch their backs.

It was a growing town with storefront buildings lining both sides of Main Street. It contained nearly all the services that El Vaquero didn't yet have, but desperately needed — a general store, post office, telegraph office, fire station, and a sheriff's department located in the front section of their jailhouse.

Ethan's boots ate up the covered porch leading from the tethering post to the front door of the sheriff's office. Wanted posters were nailed to the weathered log columns holding up the porch roof. One of them looked fresher than the others.

Ethan halted in shock at the face of the woman staring back at him. It was none other than his wife. Her name was typed in capital letters beneath her sketch. *ANNABELLE LANE: Wanted for Robbery.* A thousand dollar reward was listed for any information leading to her arrest.

"Whoa!" Jameson came to stand beside him. "That's not

something I was expecting to see. Were you?" He shoved back his Stetson and gave Ethan a hard once-over.

"No." Ethan was tempted to tear down the poster, but he didn't want to wake the deputy who was asleep on the other side of the porch. The lawman was a young fellow he'd never seen before. His chair was tipped back on two legs, and his head was resting against the wall.

He forced his hand back to his side, though his fingers were still itching to rip away the poster. "I can explain, but we need to leave," he announced in terse undertones. "Now!"

"She's a beauty, isn't she?" The legs of the deputy's chair came down on the porch with a resounding clatter. Apparently, he'd not been sleeping after all, just resting with his eyes closed. "Hard to believe she's a thief." He stood and stretched a kink out of his back. "Her poster arrived in the mail just this morning. If you're bounty hunters, feel free to take a copy of it with you. I have plenty more inside." He angled his head at the clapboard building behind him. The door was resting ajar.

"You mind if we take this one and be on our way?" Ethan pointed his thumb at the one nailed to the porch column.

The young deputy shrugged. "Help yourself and good luck on finding her. Shouldn't be too hard if she's in the area. That's a face no man will forget."

He was right. Something heavy shifted in Ethan's chest at the gravity of the position his wife was in. His mind raced to recall the number of men who'd come in contact with her. The stagecoach driver was one of them, though he might or might not pass through the area again anytime soon. The stage company often switched out their drivers. Then there was Garth Swingler, who now served as a range rider at Ford Ranch. Ethan would like to think the cowboy could be trusted, but there was no telling what a poor man might do for a thousand dollars. Garth was a cowboy he'd be watching.

Jameson kept his silence, merely tipping his hat and muttering, "Good day," to the deputy.

"God speed!" The deputy lifted his hand respectfully as Ethan and Jameson returned to their horses.

"Now, what?" Jameson eyed him sharply as they untethered and mounted up.

"I need to hire an attorney. My wife is innocent." Ethan eyed the hard-packed dirt street, remembering an attorney's shingle hanging on a building somewhere in this dusty town. At the moment, though, he couldn't recall its exact location.

"Are you sure about that, brother?"

"Very sure." His jaw tightened. "I would bank my life on the fact that there's not a dishonest bone in her body." He proceeded to give Jameson the short version of her tale about Dale Allard Featherfall. "She told me about her troubles early on, but I always felt there was more to it," he concluded. "She doesn't understand what he wants from her. All we know is that we're dealing with a scoundrel of the worst sort. No honest man would've ever tried to strong-arm a woman into marrying him in the first place, much less pay a steady stream of mercenaries to hound her." He shook his head. "Or ransack her home."

"It does seem suspicious that he waited this long to raise a hue and cry about this supposed robbery." Jameson lifted his hat to run a hand through his sun-bleached brown waves. "He wants something from her alright."

"No jest. But, what?"

"Let me see the poster again." Jameson held out his hand.

Ethan danced Ranger closer to pass it over, patting the stallion's neck to keep him calm. His horse was more accustomed to herding cattle than he was clip-clopping his way down busy city streets.

"Here we go." Jameson tapped one long finger against the

bottom of the Wanted poster. "There's the list of stolen items."

"This I've got to hear." Ethan raised his eyebrows.

"Good thing you're sitting down, because there are some very weighty items on here."

"Such as?"

"An indeterminate number of finely embroidered linens and wall hangings."

"Is this a joke?"

"I'm afraid not. I'm reading it word for word. It says here that a Mr. Dale Allard Featherfall purchased her family's estate and every item in it, per the sales agreement. Before Miss Lane moved off the property, she unlawfully took with her the following items." Jameson continued to run his finger down the page. "In addition to the linens and wall hangings, here is the rest of the list: An ancient leather-bound book of poetry, six custom-tailored gowns imported from Paris, a collection of classical paintings, a ruby ring, and gold watch."

Ethan latched on to the last item. "I've seen the gold watch."

"Have you now?" Jameson studied him with an expression that was hard to read.

"It doesn't mean she stole it," he growled in her defense. "She said it belonged to her father. She keeps it displayed right out in the open on the dresser in our bedroom. Not exactly the actions of a guilty person."

"What about the other items?"

Ethan shook his head. "Other than the watch, she owns a few pretty dresses. I have no idea if they are from Paris, London, or Timbuktu. She didn't arrive in town with any paintings or jewelry."

"She could have sold them before she left Atlanta."

Wondering whose side Jameson was on, Ethan shook his head again. "It is my belief she wouldn't have sold anything that wasn't hers to sell. It's an all-around flimsy accusation." He was having a hard time believing that the shyster who'd purchased her family home didn't believe Annabelle had the right to leave it with the clothes on her back and a few mementoes of her past life. No one in their right mind would call it stealing.

"After meeting Annabelle, I happen to agree with your assessment of her." Jameson returned the poster. "Something else that strikes me as strange is how much money this Mr. Featherfall..." he paused and snorted. "Begging your pardon. I'm having trouble repeating his name with a straight face."

Ethan barked out a laugh. "That makes two of us."

"At any rate, this scoundrel has already spent more on mercenary bandits than the value of the goods he claims were stolen. If you add in the thousand dollar reward, it makes even less sense."

"Which brings me back to my wish to hire an attorney, if we can find one that I can afford."

"I know just the man," Jameson offered matter-of-factly.

"Do tell!"

"Indeed. His name is Andrew Emerson, Esquire. He's a friend of the family," he explained vaguely. "He also happens to be the fellow who handled your application for a mail-order bride. He serves in proxy for The Western Moon Agency."

"Well, I'll be!" If the attorney's services proved affordable, Ethan would be working with a man well versed in the mail-order bride business. What a lucky coincidence!

"I'm not finished." Jameson held up a finger. "If I understood your contract correctly, all legal matters concerning your bride during the first ninety days of your marriage are covered by the fees you already paid."

Unbelievable! Ethan couldn't remember reading anything of the sort in his application. Then again, he couldn't remember much about the application with any clarity right now.

He lifted the reins of his horse. "Take me to him."

Annabelle paced the U-shaped walkway around the four-poster bed in the Fords' second-story guest room. Ethan had been gone for hours. He should have been back by now.

A light knock sounded on the door.

"Come in," she called, feeling like her nerves were about to snap.

Paloma peeked her head around the door. "Oh, dear!" she murmured. "I was hoping you were getting some rest." She bore a small wooden tray with two glasses of tea resting in the center of it. Setting it on a trestle table beneath the bay window, she motioned for Annabelle to join her in the cozy nook. Not only did it overlook the front yard, a body could see for miles across the plateau up here.

"I can't rest until Ethan gets back." Annabelle waved helplessly at the earthen road leading up to the house. "I've brought nothing but trouble into his life, and now he's out there somewhere, for all we know, being chased by the same bandits who..." She gulped, unable to finish the sentence as dread pooled in her belly.

"Then they'll wish they'd picked a different target by the time he's done with them," the motherly woman assured. "Ethan doesn't mess around when it comes to protecting and defending those he cares for."

"I'm not so sure I fall into that group," Annabelle returned bitterly. "We haven't been married for very long, and—"

"Nonsense! You're all that man can think about. I've never seen anyone so besotted."

Annabelle felt her cheeks turn red.

"Please." Paloma motioned to the overstuffed chair on the other side of the table where she was sitting. "Sit."

Annabelle moved across the room to take a tentative seat on the edge of the chair. She remained poised to spring back to her feet at any second.

"Your husband is many things, my dear, not the least of which is the best smelling range rider on our payroll." Mrs. Ford gave her a knowing smirk as she smoothed her bright skirts over her knees. She was wearing one of her favorite white cotton blouses embroidered with summer flowers at the neck and sleeves. "The other fellows tease him rather mercilessly about his new, fresh scent, calling it the married man smell."

"Say it isn't so!" Annabelle hadn't intended to cause Ethan yet more trouble. "What does he say?"

"Nothing. He ignores them like they're gnats. The look he gets on his face, though, is very telling."

"What does it tell you?" Annabelle asked quickly.

"That he would move heaven or earth to please his new bride without a single care about what others think."

His new bride, as opposed to his old one? The burst of hope her words inspired in Annabelle's chest was soon replaced by more doubts. "I want with all of my heart to believe what you say, but I'm not convinced he wanted to marry me in the first place."

"No one held a gun to his head, love."

"Actually, there were several guns firing over his head upon his arrival to the church."

"Fair enough, but I think you know what I meant." Paloma rested her elbow on the table, fixing Annabelle with a curious look. "Why do you think he didn't want to marry you?"

"He let it slip once that the whole mail-order bride contract was Jameson's idea." She swallowed the lump rising in her throat. "I believe it had more to do with settling this town with families than anything else."

"Hmm." Paloma pursed her lips. "I can't say exactly why Ethan agreed to the whole proposition. What I can say is this. His current interest in you has nothing to do with pioneering towns. He truly cares for you."

Annabelle turned her face away from the window to meet the woman's gaze. "Then where is he now?"

"On his way." Paloma nodded at the window. "He'll be back before nightfall. I guarantee it."

Annabelle both longed for and dreaded her husband's return. "I sure hope so," she whispered.

"Regardless of the hour he makes it back, you'll be staying here the night. You and him both." Paloma's voice was firm.

In the same room? Annabelle caught her breath. *Together?* Butterflies churned in her stomach at the realization that even the woman Ethan looked up to like a mother assumed that they'd already consummated their marriage.

"That is very kind of you," she murmured breathlessly, trying to think of an excuse as to why they could not share a room.

"It's the least we can do to help. Your husband made it clear he didn't want to take you home until he got the cabin cleaned up some."

And perhaps the baby cradle and trunks in the loft relocated. Annabelle squeezed her eyelids shut, trying to block out the memory of the woman's clothing and all the baby items she'd stumbled across.

"I'll find a way to repay you." She reopened her eyes, peering past damp lids to meet Paloma's gaze. "Hopefully, with fresh produce. I was supposed to start planting a garden this morning, before I was so viciously interrupted."

Paloma frowned. "This isn't about trading favors, Annabelle. You're part of the family now. There's nothing Ethan wouldn't do for us in return. In time, we hope to earn the same loyalty from you."

Annabelle stared at her in amazement, surprised that the woman would place any value on the loyalty of a mere mail-order bride. "I am no longer a person of any social consequence. The Lane legacy died with my father. What is left of it is fast being squandered by an unscrupulous tradesman. My good opinion is quite literally worth nothing." Her voice hitched with misery.

"On that, we will have to disagree," her hostess returned firmly. "I know for a fact that your husband disagrees. He's done little else but sing your praises ever since he brought you home. He is enamored with your cooking, cleaning, singing, and everything else you do."

"My voice?" Annabelle had never sung for her husband before.

"He said you were singing one evening when he returned home and he waited outside on the front porch until you finished."

"Oh, my!" she murmured faintly. "Why would he do a thing like that?"

"Because he was utterly enthralled by your voice. He said it sounded like an angel chorus. The last thing he wanted to do was interrupt you before you finished."

Annabelle caught her lower lip between her teeth, flushing with confusion. If her husband was as enamored with her as Paloma claimed, then why had he waited so long to tell her about his first wife and the baby he'd lost?

"How long have you known Ethan?" She fiddled with the sleeve of the clean white blouse the woman had insisted she borrow. Her fingers traveled over the thick bandage covering her elbow beneath the fabric. Though it was only a minor abrasion, Paloma had wrapped a healing poultice around it.

"A little over four years. My boys traveled all the way to the mountains of New Mexico to recruit him."

"Did he leave anyone behind?" Annabelle wasn't entirely sure how to phrase the question. "A family? Loved ones?"

"No." Paloma's voice turned sad. "He is the only one left in his family. That's why it didn't take much convincing for him to join our growing community here in El Vaquero."

There was the clattering of hoofbeats outside the window.

Paloma and Annabelle whirled around to peer outside.

"There he is, my dear!" Paloma reached over to pat her arm. "Did I not say he would return to you safe and sound?" She hurriedly stacked the empty tea glasses on her tray and stood. "Ethan will be parched from his journey. I'll bring up a fresh round of tea shortly."

"Thank you." Annabelle stood to give her shoulders a quick squeeze. "For everything."

"I'll bring something to eat, as well."

"That would be marvelous." Annabelle gave her a wobbly smile. Her ears were already tuning in to the pounding of feet on the stairs.

Shortly after Paloma left the room, the doorway was filled with a much larger frame. Ethan had arrived.

His hat was grasped in one hand, leaving a crease around his dark hair where it had rested.

Their gazes locked and held for an extended moment.

Then Annabelle's face crumpled. "Ethan." She raised and lowered her hands. There were so many questions burning in her mind.

He stepped across the threshold, kicking the door shut behind him. "Are you in any pain?" He traversed the room to stand in front of her, eyeing her anxiously.

"Only here." She pressed a hand to her heart.

"Did you fall?" He lifted her hand and lightly palpated the area with the pads of his fingers.

"I'm referring to my heart, Ethan." She steeled herself against the gentleness of his touch, needing to know the truth before their marriage could go any further. If he truly didn't want to be married, this was the time for them to end things — now, before he incurred any more damage to his property or other losses on her behalf.

"Oh." He lowered his hand, looking wary.

"I know you didn't want me up in the loft," she continued in a rush. "You made it very clear you didn't want me up there, and now I know why."

His gaze burned into hers. "First of all, I am more grateful than words can express that you found sanctuary there. If you think for one second that I wish otherwise, you couldn't be more wrong. Second of all, I was meaning to tell you about everything you found up there." He paused a beat. "In time."

"When?" she cried. "After our next kiss? After you took me to bed?"

"No!" His voice was so harsh that she jumped. "I would have told you before then. You deserve no less."

She nodded, grateful to hear it as tears spilled weakly down her cheeks. "Who was she?"

"My wife." A pained expression crossed his strong features. "I lost her while she struggled to bear our son. I lost both of them. The only reason you and I have not talked about it before now is because it's not something I find easy to talk about." He glanced away.

"Because you still love her?"

"A part of me will always care for her, Annabelle. She was a good woman, one who was far too delicate for mountain life. Knowing what I did for a living, I should have never asked her to marry me. That is the part that is difficult to talk about. I have regrets that I will carry to my grave."

The pain in his voice was so wretched that Annabelle couldn't resist reaching out to touch his arm. "What happened to them is not your fault, any more than what happened to my family is mine."

"It doesn't feel that way, Annabelle. It was my job to protect them, and I failed."

"How?" *Good gracious!* The man was so honorable that he couldn't see past his own honorableness.

"She was bedridden most of the time she was in the family way. I should have moved her to a bigger town where she could have received better care." He waved a hand helplessly. "Where there was a midwife, at least."

"And paid for it, how?"

"I don't know. I would have figured something out."

"Oh, Ethan!" Despite Annabelle's many misgivings about where they stood with each other, she stepped closer to slide her arms around his middle. "You're a range rider. It's your livelihood. I suspect your first wife understood that when she married you. I'm going to go out on a limb and say she also probably understood the risks...and considered you worth every one of them." She turned her face into his chest. "As I do."

Ethan's arms came around her. "Those are the kindest words anyone has ever spoken to me. Thank you." He hugged her tighter.

Her heart swelled at the knowledge that she'd given him comfort. "I'm sorry about everything else," she muttered after a while. More tears seeped from her eyelids. "All the trouble I've brought you. All the damage your cabin suffered today because of me. I wouldn't blame you one bit if you annulled our marriage and sent me away."

"What?" He yanked her closer still. "What makes you think I want an annulment?"

She felt a full-body flush rise to the surface of her skin. *In for a penny.* She was tired of walking around on eggshells. Life was too short. "Because you sleep upstairs. Because we're running out of time to consummate our marriage according to our contract. Because of the cradle I found in the loft today. Because of the danger I'm in and the danger I've unwittingly kept you in since the day we exchanged our vows."

He gave a disbelieving chuckle and buried his face against the side of her neck. "I've been sleeping upstairs because we were strangers when we met. You deserved to be wooed and courted, not callously manhandled. I wanted you to be ready to be with me when it finally happened. To want it as much as I do."

To want it as much as I do. A shaky laugh escaped Annabelle at how wrong she'd been about him. It was a relief to learn that the distance he'd kept from her had nothing to do with the chests in the loft. Rather, it had everything to do with the caliber of man he was. A perfect gentleman, despite his rugged appearance.

"What's so funny?" he growled.

She reveled in the accelerated beat of his heart beneath her cheek. "This morning when I was making your bedroll, I hugged your pillow so you would fall asleep surrounded by the scent of rosewater."

"Did you now?" His voice grew husky.

"I was hoping it would be more subtle and ladylike than leaving a written invitation for you to join me downstairs."

"I reckon that answers the question of where I'll be staying tonight."

A knock on the guest room door made him groan. "Unfortunately, very few people in this family understand the concept of newlyweds." He lifted his head and raised his voice. "It means go away and leave us alone!"

There was a brief pause before Paloma trilled, "I'll just

leave your tray of refreshments outside the door." There was laughter in her voice. And understanding.

"By all that is holy!" he muttered. Turning nearly as red as Annabelle, he dropped his arms from around her and went to retrieve the tray. "If I could guarantee your safety there, I would return with you to our cabin right this second."

It was a sober reminder of the bigger issues at hand.

As he set the tray of tea and sandwiches on the table in the window alcove, she moved to the nightstand to fetch her father's watch. As much as she hated the thought of parting with such a precious item, she knew it was the only way she could contribute to the repairs their home needed. "I don't know if this is enough to cover the damage to the doors and windows. It should help, though." She walked toward him with the watch outstretched. "I'll need you to help me find a buyer for it, but it's gold, so it has to be worth something."

"Absolutely not!" Ethan's voice was so fierce that her feet churned to a halt. The watch slid from her grasp. She stared in agony as it clattered to the floor. The clasp that had been sealed shut for so long flew open. A piece broke loose and fell out. "Oh, no!" She slid to her knees on a sob. "Oh, no, no, no, no, no! It's the last thing I own of any value." She scrambled blindly along the floor in search of the broken piece.

"No. It's not." Ethan's hands gently grasped her shoulders and tugged her upright. "You are far more valuable to me than a watch." He gave her a gentle shake. "Do you hear me, Annabelle?"

She blinked to bring his face back into focus. Then she nodded. Pointing dazedly at the floor, she babbled, "I need to find all the pieces. Maybe we can have it fixed."

He nodded and squatted down beside her to help her search. Her fingers closed around the watch. Snatching it up, she examined it carefully, but it was not immediately apparent what had broken loose. The face of the watch was intact. There wasn't a single crack in the glass.

"What in the world?" Ethan leaned over farther to pick something up. "This must have been what fell out when you dropped it." He raised a folded piece of paper between two fingers.

She reached for it greedily, depositing her father's watch in his hand for safekeeping. "It looks like a note," she breathed. Weakness coursed through her limbs as she unfolded the paper. The message it contained was in her father's handwriting.

My dearest daughter,
If you are reading this, then I did not make it back home.

It was like hearing a voice from the dead. Tears rolled unchecked down Annabelle's cheeks while she read her father's final words. He described the railroad spur he'd invested in. It was one he expected to become a major water stop and cattle shipping point in Texas. He'd left the investment papers in the hands of an attorney friend to manage in his absence. Ever since his passing, it had been held in a trust in her name that would become her dowry the day she wed.

"Ah, Ethan?" she choked, raising her damp gaze to his.

"What is it, darlin'?"

"I think you own a railroad spur."

His dark eyebrows rose. "Come again?"

She wordlessly handed him the slip of paper.

He was silent for a long time, shaking his head as he read and reread the message.

"Say something," she begged.

He handed the note back to her. "I always knew there was something more to these bandits."

She bit her lower lip. "Mr. Featherfall is a very wealthy

man, which means he wouldn't have pursued me this hard if there wasn't a lot of money involved. I reckon it means that you, too, are now a very wealthy man."

"We'll find out soon enough." Her husband's expression was hard to read.

She glanced toward the window at the fading sunlight. "I don't know what the chances are of making it to El Gato before the telegraph office closes." There was an address listed on the letter for her father's friend, an attorney working in Houston. It shouldn't prove too difficult to reach out to him.

"Not tonight, Annabelle." Ethan held out his hand to her. "We have dinner waiting over by the window. Afterward, I'm going to prove to you just how much I want to stay married to you, whether or not this railroad spur pans out."

Chapter 8: Riders on the Range
ANNABELLE

Next morning

Annabelle awoke in a tangle of bed linens that made her blush, though the spot beside her was empty. She sat up, blinking in the morning sunlight, wondering where Ethan was.

"I'm over here, darlin'." His low and caressing voice rumbled from the direction of the window.

She blinked again and found him standing in a ray of sunshine, dressed for the day. One arm was propped against the wall while he watched the activity outside the window. She could hear voices and the whinny of horses.

"What's going on?" She eyed his plaid shirt and denim trousers. They were freshly laundered and pressed. Someone must have brought him a change of clothing from the cabin.

"We're leaving."

"Leaving!" She rubbed her eyes and looked at him again. "When?"

"Now." He pushed away from the wall, scooping up her travel bag from one of the chairs. "As soon as you get changed, that is." Tossing the bag beside her on the bed, he leaned in to nuzzle the edge of her mouth. "I hope you rested well."

Tugging the flaps of her robe more tightly around her, she blushed from the roots of her hair to her toes that were curling beneath the sheets. "I feel wonderful. Better than I have in a long time."

"Good." The smile he gave her was very male and very satisfied.

"You look smug." She chuckled, despite the shyness sweeping through her.

"If I am, it's entirely your fault, darlin'." He waggled his eyebrows at her. "I'm married to a highfalutin southern belle who spent half the night making a lowly range rider the happiest man in the state of Texas. So you'll just have to forgive me if I'm feeling a little smug this morning."

"And cocky," she added, opening her travel bag to find a clean gown inside. It was her pink one — the laciest, frilliest dress she owned. "Where might you be taking me in my best dress?" Visions of boat rides on the river and picnics in the park flashed through her mind.

"Some place safe." His expression sobered. "You're a wanted woman, darlin'."

"What about the railroad spur?"

"Jameson and our attorney in El Gato will look into it while we're away."

She frowned as she slid her feet over the side of the bed and padded barefoot to the washbasin. "How long will we be gone?" She splashed water on her face and patted it dry with a towel.

"Until the wanted posters are taken down and the warrant for your arrest is withdrawn."

She spun around with a squeak of alarm. "My what?"

He grimaced. "There's a warrant out for your arrest."

"How long have you known about this?"

"Since Jameson and I rode into El Gato yesterday. We saw the wanted poster, then met with an attorney who additionally informed us about your outstanding arrest warrant."

"And you're just now telling me?" She gaped at the bed where they had spent such an idyllic night. He'd known about the warrant the whole time, but he'd never let on.

"I reckon I am."

"Why?" she asked faintly.

"Because you'd already been through so much. I figured you deserved one last decent night of sleep before..." He shrugged.

"Before we go on the run." Together, it seemed.

"More or less."

"What about your job and your home?" she protested.

"My job and *our* home," he stressed the word *our* with a pointed look at her, "will be waiting for us when we get back." He moved to the window to look out again. "Hurry, darlin'. We don't have much time."

"Why did you bring my best dress?" she grumbled. It would've taken far less time to don her work gown.

"Because I like seeing you in it, but that's not what you'll be wearing today. Take it out of the bag and look underneath it. That's what you'll be wearing."

She did as he suggested and tugged out a pair of trousers and a faded plaid shirt. It was like the one he was wearing, but smaller. "You want me to wear trousers?"

"It'll be easier to ride a horse in them." He produced a Stetson and zinged it across the room. It landed on the bed next to her. "You'd best pin up your hair and hide it beneath that."

The details finally clicked into place for her. She'd be dressing like him, a range rider. "I may very well be married to the smartest man in Texas," she sighed, sending him a grateful look.

"Still feeling smug," he joked as she swiftly donned the borrowed outfit and pinned her hair beneath the hat.

As she scanned the floor for her lace-up boots, he slid a pair of cowboy boots in her direction with his toe. "This is what you'll be wearing today, darlin'. They're hand-me-downs from Lance. His mother never got rid of them after he grew out of them."

"And where might we range riders be going?" She took a few steps to practice her swagger.

He grinned at her antics. "Out on the range. You're about to get a first-hand taste of what it's like to tend the herds and protect them from predators — both the four-legged kind and the two-legged kind."

"So, we'll be hiding in plain sight."

"That we will."

"It's a clever idea."

"Then you can thank Jameson for coming up with it. I was initially in favor of running with you as far from here as possible. After we debated our options, however, he convinced me you'd be safer within the protection of our own range riders."

She shivered as doubts crept in. "How can we be sure that none of them will turn me in to collect the thousand dollars?"

"Because they are loyal employees. The Fords and me have personally vetted every one of them except Garth Swingler."

"He won't give me up." She shook her head vehemently. "He idolizes you and risked his hide to protect mine on our way to the church."

"We are hoping his loyalties remain strong." Ethan's expression was noncommittal. "We'll be keeping a close eye on him until we're certain he's one hundred percent on our side."

"You doubt him, eh?" She tossed her father's watch inside her travel bag. Her father's note, however, she was reluctant to bring along.

"We've been unsuccessful in uncovering any information about him so far. Can't find his hometown, birth records, or any living relatives. He's a blank slate, which most likely means he's living under an assumed name."

She drew a sharp breath. "Does that mean he's dirty?"

"Not necessarily. Plenty of cowpokes go by nicknames and the like. Sometimes they earn them from their reputations. Other times, they fabricate the names in an effort to keep a low profile."

"Thank you for the warning," she sighed. "I'll be sure to keep my guard up around him."

"Thank you, darlin'. That's all I'm asking for."

"Well, I happen to have two more requests before we depart."

He raised his eyebrows at her as he strode across the room to pick up her travel bag.

She waved her father's note at him. "I don't want to lose this. Is there a safe place to store it while we're gone?"

"Normally, I'd say memorize it and burn it."

At her gasp of shock, he continued, "But since it holds sentimental value—"

"*Great* sentimental value," she cut in.

"Yes. That. For this reason, I'd recommend either leaving it with Jameson to tuck inside the family vault or deliver it to our attorney in El Gato. Your choice."

"Leave it with our attorney." She didn't have to think twice. She had no wish to make the Fords a target of her enemies.

"Good choice." He reached for the note. "If you'd prefer, I'll do the hand off."

"Please." As she relinquished the note to him, she slid her hands up his chest to twine them around his neck. "Now, for my last request. A kiss."

"Yes, ma'am." Still gripping her travel bag, Ethan dipped

his head to capture her mouth in the tenderest of kisses. It made her insides glow like a brand new dawn.

Without warning, the door to the guest room flew open. As Annabelle and Ethan's heads swung toward the door, Lance announced at the top of his lungs, "Found them!" To the startled couple in front of him, he exploded, "Great balls of fire! The world is coming to an end, and you two are up here kissing. Kissing!"

"My wife and I were about ready to make an appearance," Ethan informed him loftily, nudging Annabelle toward the door.

"No, you weren't." Lance stepped in their path to halt them. "You're two range riders who are about to join up with the next patrol. It won't do us a lick of good to have her outside," he jammed a thumb in Annabelle's direction, "glowing like a bonfire, just because you're incapable of keeping your cowboy hands, mouth, and mind off of her in front of a federal marshal!"

Annabelle started to giggle, but Ethan's expression stopped her. "What's this about a federal marshal?"

"Your guess is as good as mine. All I can tell you is there's a man outside claiming to be one, and he's got a whole posse of armed men riding with him."

"What does he want?" Ethan demanded.

"He says he wants to have a word with you about a certain bride on a certain Wanted poster."

"And so it begins," Ethan muttered with a regretful glance at Annabelle. To Lance, he demanded, "How can we be sure he's a real federal marshal?"

"Other than his badge, we can't. He showed up out of nowhere. If we'd known he was coming, we'd have made sure you left last night."

Annabelle was selfishly glad they hadn't known about the

marshal. Otherwise, she and Ethan might never have gotten to enjoy their swift, impromptu honeymoon.

"Lance is right, darlin'." Ethan stepped closer to her to brush his mouth against her temple. "For the next several hours, days, and maybe weeks, your safety will hinge directly on your ability to pass yourself off as a range rider."

She momentarily closed her eyes to absorb his gentle caress. If everything he said was true, it might be a long time before he was at liberty to touch her again.

"A junior one." Lance's voice was scoffing. "She's too tiny for anything else." He beckoned at them to follow him down the stairs. Glancing back to catch Annabelle's eye, he explained, "That means if any other rider says jump, you jump. If they want you to fetch something, you fetch it. If one of them tells you to—"

"I understand," she interrupted flatly.

When Ethan moved around them in the foyer to open the front door for her, Lance stepped between them. "Huh-uh. You let it slam in her face from now on, Vasquez. Are you picking up what I'm putting down?"

Ethan's dark gaze glittered so coldly at the younger cowboy that, for a moment, Annabelle feared he was going to strike him. Then he nodded. "I hear your loud and jangly voice."

"Then hand over her travel bag. You shouldn't be seen with anything that belongs to her. She shouldn't either, which is why I'll be having everything in it transferred to a proper saddle bag."

Ethan shoved it none too gently at him. Slapping open the door, he stomped outside to the porch.

He scanned the front lawn, taking in the presence of the federal marshal on his horse. He and a trio of mounted deputies were waiting in the circle driveway in front of the farmhouse.

Ignoring them, he bellowed to the range riders milling around the yard. "Mount up! It's time to ride."

None of them moved. A few of them angled their heads respectfully at the marshal, or the man posing as one. He was silently holding up a hand for their attention.

"Mr. Ethan Vasquez." He leaped to the ground and handed the reins of his horse to the rider nearest him. "If I may have a brief word with you." He looked as cool as a cucumber in black trousers, a pressed white shirt, and a leather Stetson. The gold star pinned to his shirt glinted in the morning sun.

Ethan gave the man a rigid nod. To his men, he snarled, "Well, what are you waiting for? He wants to speak to me, not to you. Now get back to work." He'd never before seen so many men move so quickly, nor had he ever been prouder of them.

Out of the corner of his eye, he watched Garth Swingler lead a horse up to Annabelle. Punching her lightly on the shoulder, as if they were comrades, he handed over the reins. To his relief, Annabelle mounted without a hitch, though she was unaccustomed to riding astride. She was going to be saddle sore something awful come morning, but it couldn't be helped.

"I'm Turner King, U.S. Federal Marshal." Mr. King held out a hand, watching Ethan closely.

He turned his back on his wife to give the marshal's hand a firm shake. "Pleased to meet you. It sounds like you already know who I am." He dropped his hands to his sides. "If this is about the robbery, we are mighty grateful you rode all the way out here to look into it."

He figured it was best to pretend like he was cooperating with the law in every way. Even if the man was who he said he was, Ethan and the Fords had no way of knowing how much he and his posse had been influenced by Mr. Featherfall. Or paid off, for that matter. It was prudent to assume the worst while protecting Annabelle's location at all costs. For now, at any rate.

"You can imagine my shock when I found out I'd wed a woman with a bounty on her head." He spat on the ground in disgust.

"We were just as surprised," one of the marshal's companions chortled. "It ain't often we get to arrest a woman!"

Ethan's blood boiled at how eager the young lawman sounded.

Mr. King angled his head at the other horsemen. "I brought a few local deputies with me. Figured you might be more comfortable talking to me if you recognized the men in my party."

Ethan nodded, though he didn't see a single familiar face.

"Is your wife here?" The marshal glanced around the front yard soberly. "We were hoping to have a word with her, as well."

"No, sir. She plumb took off." Ethan gave an exaggerated wave of his hands, feigning exasperation.

"Any idea when she'll return, Mr. Vasquez?"

He shook his head, curling his upper lip. "I can't rightly say if she'll ever return." He was careful with his statements, skirting the line between the truth and calculated omissions.

"I am sorry to hear it, Mr. Vasquez. With mail-order brides in such high demand in the wilderness, it's not surprising that these agencies occasionally let a bad apple through their ranks. I reckon it isn't easy to match the supply to the demand."

"Probably not, sir. All the same, I'll be demanding a refund if she doesn't come back."

The rest of the marshal's questions were quick and straightforward. "When was the last time you saw your wife, Mr. Vasquez?"

Again, he pretended to ponder the question. "I'd appreciate it if you'd quit calling her that."

"Weren't the two of you legally wed?"

"Yes, but my contract says I have ninety days to make sure everything is ship-shape. Otherwise, I can cancel it, which I am strongly considering."

Mr. King nodded. "Very well. When was the last time you saw the mail-order bride who was sent to you?"

"I see her everywhere, sir." Ethan didn't see why he couldn't have a little fun playing the part of the hotheaded Mexican who'd been slighted. "In my nightmares. In my—"

"I understand, Mr. Vasquez. What I was referring to was the last time you physically saw her." After a pause, he added, "In the flesh."

Trying not to think about their impromptu honeymoon in the Fords' guest suite last night, Ethan pursed his lips thoughtfully. "We-e-e-ell, I saw her right before I left for work yesterday morning. She kissed me and pretended like everything was alright. That was right before those scallawags tore through my cabin like it was Armageddon and robbed me blind. For all I know, she was in on it. Took everything of value."

"Which was what, exactly?"

Ethan spread his hands. "My best hunting rifle and the gold watch Annabelle gave me as a wedding gift. Said it belonged to her father. Bah!" He spat on the ground again. "Bet she and her cronies intended to take it back all along. Talk about a gift with strings attached!"

The marshal's gaze sharpened at the mention of the gold watch. "Were you aware that a gold watch is on the list of items she reportedly stole from a Mr. Dale Allard Featherfall back in Atlanta?"

Ethan grimaced to avoid smirking at the crook's hideous name. "Can't say I'm surprised. It's starting to look as if everything that witch told me was a lie."

The marshal's sharp look made him wonder if he'd overdone the venom. "Do you mind if we search your cabin, Mr. Vasquez?"

If he had to ask, he must not be in possession of a search warrant. "Not at all, but what are you looking for? She's long gone, I tell you, and I ain't too sure she's coming back."

"Clues, Mr. Vasquez. Any clue as to where she might have high-tailed it."

Ethan shrugged. "The front and back doors are both kicked off their hinges. You can march right in and search for clues whenever you please."

"We'd like to take a look at it today, Mr. Vasquez. Our plan is to head there just as soon as we finish speaking with the Fords."

Ethan glared balefully at no one in particular. "Well, you know where to find me if you have any more questions."

"And that is?"

"On patrol, sir. I never leave this here property, except for an occasional supply run to El Gato." He was thoroughly enjoying speaking in vagaries that sounded like solid information, knowing he was telling the lawman next to nothing he didn't already know or could easily guess.

Turner King slowly nodded. "That will be all, Mr. Vasquez. Like you said, we know where to find you if we have any more questions."

"A good day to you, sir." Ethan tipped his hat at him and his posse, not planning on being available the next time they called.

JOVIE GRACE

Garth rode closer to Annabelle as the first of the Fords' longhorn herds came into sight. "Pretty scraggly, ain't they?"

"I, ah...yes. I reckon they are a bit on the slender side." She caught her breath in wonder at the beautiful creatures. Though they were far from fat, she would have never employed the term scraggly to describe them.

They weren't like the cattle back in Georgia. Their most prominent feature was their horns, which stretched a good seven to eight feet from tip to tip. Grazing in clusters across the field of scruffy grasses and Joshua trees, they were truly magnificent beasts.

To her, their slender frames didn't take away from their beauty. Her gaze swept over a sleek caramel colored one, then a black-and-white spotted one, and finally a reddish-brown one with a white nose and white legs.

"Want to know why they're so skinny?" Garth pressed.

"Yes, indeed." She was curious to know the answer.

"They were brought to Mexico by the conquistadors, then driven north to other settlements. Some of them escaped. Others were turned loose for reasons we may never know. They've wandered around feral ever since, surviving both famines and droughts. Their suffering has made them one of the hardiest breeds, albeit the skinniest. Always scavenging for food, but free as birds while doing it."

"Until now," Annabelle finished in a low voice. From what she understood, the Fords were wholly building their herds by rounding up the wild longhorns.

"Until now." Garth's lips turned downward in disapproval, which made no sense. He wouldn't have a job if the Fords weren't so busy rounding up cattle. His normal grin returned so quickly that she wondered if it was a trick of the sunlight to imagine he was anything other than pleased with his employers.

Either that, or she was imagining things that weren't there, due to Ethan's warning to be cautious around Garth.

OVER THE NEXT MONTH AND A HALF, ANNABELLE learned the ins and outs of range riding, thanks to Ethan, Garth, and the other fellows. Once the saddle soreness wore off, she was able to relax and enjoy her newest adventure. She became more adept at wielding her pistol, even allowing Garth to teach her how to properly twirl it.

The young cowboy stuck to her like a cocklebur, never once wavering in his loyalty to her. He was so patient with her while learning the business of range riding that she hoped, in time, he would earn Ethan's approval. It was all he seemed to want.

"I don't know what's come over me," she moaned, clutching her belly one morning.

"Probably something you ate." Garth nodded sagely. "You'll eventually hack it up like a cow chewing his cud. Then you'll feel better."

"Thanks," she muttered in misery, wanting to slap him for his excessive cheerfulness. Now was not the time to spill sunshine all over her while she felt like she was dying. She was relieved when he finally took off and left her alone for a while, probably needing a break from the sound of her retching.

Ethan continued to drive them and the herds forward despite her bouts of sickness. More than once, she had to slide off the back of her horse to empty the contents of her stomach into the nearest bush. Lightheadedness set in as her body became stripped of its fluids.

"Mr. Vasquez says you need to keep drinking." Garth reappeared with a plump skin sloshing with fluid. He shoved it at her.

She took one sniff, and her stomach did a crazy little flip-flop. "I can't." It was cider. She pushed it away. "It smells putrid." Oh, how she longed for a sip of plain old water — the cooler, the better!

The sun rose higher overhead, beating oppressively down on them.

Garth urged her again and again to drink. "Just take one sip," he begged.

"I can't bear the scent." Her mouth felt like it was full of cotton balls. "I'll just throw it right back up." *What is wrong with me?* If she didn't turn the corner soon and start getting well, she'd have to seek medical care, which would blow her cover. Any visit with a physician could end in her arrest. According to the latest updates from the Fords, her Wanted posters were circulating all the surrounding towns.

"What will it take to get you to drink again?" Garth sighed.

"Water," she bleated pitifully. "If you can find me some fresh water, I promise to guzzle it down."

"Consider it done," he vowed. "I won't return until I find you a fresh mountain stream."

She watched him dizzily as he dug in his heels and rode off. By the time he returned an hour or so later, she was close to swooning. It felt like the sun and wind were working in unison to pull every last drop of moisture from her body.

"This way!" Garth waved joyfully at her. "I found water!"

Annabelle glanced toward Ethan for approval, but his attention was on a twirl of smoke rising from the next peak. "Appears to be a brush fire," he barked to one of the range riders. "Let's take a closer look."

Knowing he would be displeased to find her missing when he returned, she wrinkled her nose at Garth. "How far it is?"

"Not far," he promised with a knowing grin in Ethan's direction. "We'll be back pronto. The boss will never know we were gone."

Shaking her head at the scolding she was sure to receive upon her return, she dug her heels into Spots' sides and followed the cowboy. He slowed his pace until she caught up so he could ride abreast of her. Then he slowed his pace even more and edged his horse in behind hers.

"Stop, Annabelle!" he commanded suddenly. His voice was low and terse.

She dizzily complied, slumping forward against the neck of her horse.

"You're not well enough to keep riding," he advised grimly. "At the risk of incurring the wrath of Mr. Vasquez, I'd like to put you on my horse and carry you the rest of the way."

"I can't leave Spots!" she gasped. Ethan would never forgive her for being so careless with his horse.

"We won't. We'll tether her to that tree in the shade up ahead and return before she has a chance to miss us."

Shade? What shade? Annabelle blinked as the world around her grew fuzzy.

She came close to swooning when Garth lifted her from her horse. "Easy does it," he soothed, placing her on his own horse and hopping on behind her. "We're almost there."

Almost where? She slumped against him, closing her eyes.

"Drink this. We don't want to lose you." The next thing she knew, a skin of water was pressed to her lips.

Oh, dear heavens! It tasted so good that she drank more than she should have. The nausea must have passed, because she no longer had the urge to choke it back up. After a few minutes, the dizziness faded, too, and her strength started to return.

"More water," she pleaded.

Garth passed the skin to her again.

As she drank, she gradually became aware of their surroundings once again. With her awareness came the realization that they weren't anywhere near Ford Ranch. She could no longer hear the bays of the longhorns and the calls of the range riders.

She straightened in the saddle. "Where are we, Garth?"

An inane sounding chuckle erupted from him. "There's something I want to show you."

She twisted around to look at him. "I asked where we're going," she repeated firmly.

"To your father's railroad spur." His silly expression evaporated and was replaced by one of pure malice. "That's your dowry, isn't it?"

Her insides grew cold. "How do you know about that?"

"Because he was foolish enough to brag about it to a fellow soldier who told someone else whom I overheard telling yet another person. I decided on the spot that I wanted to be the lucky fellow to marry his daughter and take the dowry for myself. All I had to do was find the watch where your dowry papers were stowed for safekeeping."

She shivered at how many people must have known about her dowry before she'd discovered it. "You're out of your mind!" she gasped.

"So my father claims. If I am, it's his fault for sending me off to an asylum instead of legitimizing me. He changed his tune, though, after I escaped and shared my plans to marry you. You should have seen him scrambling through your father's old books and journals to verify my claim."

"You mean Mr. Featherfall?" She scrambled to make sense of Garth's newest revelation.

"The one and only," he mocked. "He's the reason your stubborn groom and his interfering family couldn't find any record of my birth. My father made sure it was never recorded, so he could spend all these years pretending I didn't exist." His mouth twisted bitterly. "And keeping me out of his will."

"There's one thing I still don't understand." Annabelle's mind raced over all the fragments of information she'd learned during the past few months. "If you're the one who's supposed to marry me and assume ownership of the railroad spur, then why did Mr. Featherfall propose to me before I left Atlanta?"

Garth's face grew red with anger. "That's a lie!" he screeched. "You're only saying that to turn me against him, and I won't have it! I've worked too long and hard to earn his approval."

"I'm not lying!" After everything he'd suffered at his father's hands, she couldn't believe how blind he remained toward the man's true nature. "He even threatened to send debt collectors after me if I refused to marry him. That's why I left town."

"If you don't stop talking about him like that, I'll gag you," Garth declared fiercely. "My friends and I were the only ones following you. When you gave us the slip on the train, you nearly ruined everything. Father blamed me. It took hours to convince him to give me another chance."

"To fetch me back to Atlanta," she supplied, feeling sick.

"Yes."

"So he could force me to marry him. Wake up, Garth! I think you know that I'm telling you the truth."

"I said stop talking about my father like that!"

"Just listen," she begged. "He is determined to marry again so he can beget an heir, a legitimate one. Which means he never intended to keep his word to you. He's only using you to—"

A sharp pain exploded against the side of her head, and everything went black.

Chapter 9: Railroad Ties

ETHAN

Ethan gave the burning Joshua tree a hard look, then turned to scan the surrounding mountainside. *A solo tree in flames?* Something wasn't right about the scene. Tufts of dry grass waved nearby, and a rattlesnake scuttled farther beneath a boulder.

He motioned for the young range rider at his side to dismount. "Let's dig a trench around it. Doesn't need to be deep. Just wide enough to keep the flames from spreading."

In the absence of hoes and shovels, they used fallen branches and sharp stones to carve the trench. The fire blossomed into deep oranges and blues, sparks flying this way and that in the swirling breeze.

Ethan and the junior range rider had to leap around the circle, stomping out the sparks before they ignited the mounds of grass. It was several minutes before the strength of the fire consumed enough of the short, squatty tree to make it safe to kick the remaining branches to the ground. They swiftly snuffed out the flames with the heels of their boots, then kicked a layer of sand over the charred remains.

Dusting his hands, Ethan nodded for his companion to

mount up once again. Digging in their heels, they rode back to rejoin their patrol. The longhorn cattle were scattered across both sides of the mountain pass, munching and lazing around in the sun.

Out of sheer habit, Ethan's gaze searched out Annabelle. She and Garth were nowhere in sight. His next observation was that there were fewer range riders than normal guarding the perimeter. Ethan nudged his horse forward to the nearest rider. "Where is she?" he demanded harshly.

The cowboy pointed east. "We think Garth took her in that direction for water."

"You think?" Ethan snarled, his chest tightening with apprehension.

"I'm sorry, boss." The man raised and lowered his hand helplessly. "While you were putting out the first fire, another one started behind us. I reckon we were distracted, trying to prevent the whole field from going up in flames."

Ethan nodded. His crew had taken the correct course of action. Otherwise, they might have lost the entire herd. It wasn't their job to play nursemaid to one petite range rider who wasn't really a range rider.

Two unexplainable fires, instead of one. More convinced than ever that something was amiss, he raised his Stetson to run a hand through his sweaty hair while scanning the craggy terrain. *Where are you, Annabelle?* She knew better than to take off on her own. Even with Garth at her side, it was dangerous. He still hadn't finished vetting the cowboy to his satisfaction, and there was no telling when and where the next rustlers would be lurking.

He jammed his hat back on his head. "Where are the other riders?" It was an open question for anyone within hearing distance to answer.

"Out looking for her, sir," the same range rider answered.

"Carry on." Ethan dismissed the cowboy, angry at himself

for assuming Annabelle would be safe within the ranks of so many Ford Ranch employees. It only took one snake in the grass, one wolf slinking among the sheep...

Ethan didn't care if Garth Swingler had only taken his wife on the reported water run. When he finally caught up with the two of them, there was going to be a reckoning. The fellow was going to need a powerful good excuse for what he'd done to keep his job.

He wheeled Ranger east and rode to the highest peak. Pausing on the ridge, he scanned the open range ahead of him. He could see nothing but more wild grass, twisted trees, and a scattering of cacti.

A familiar whinny had him jerking the reins and digging in his heels. Unless his ears were playing tricks on him, Spots was nearby, which had to mean his wife was, as well. "Annabelle?" he shouted, knowing it wasn't wise to shout her name so loud. "Annabe-e-elle!"

Spots continued to guide him with her whinnies. They increased in urgency as he drew closer. Ethan found her tethered to a Joshua tree with a snake coiling nearby. Leaping down from Ranger, he landed with the heel of his boot on the head of the serpent, crushing it.

The spotted Mustang settled down, her flanks lathered with sweat. Both her rider and her saddle bag were missing.

Anger speared through Ethan. No one with an ounce of human decency left in them would leave a horse tethered in the sun, defenseless against predators. It was deliberately cruel.

Garth Swingler was the most likely suspect, since Annabelle would have never done anything so dastardly. Unable to think of any good reason for such behavior, Ethan tasted fear, knowing he should have listened to his gut where Garth Swingler was concerned. Something about the fellow had never set right with him. So help him, if the cowboy so much as harmed a hair on his wife's head, he might as well dig his own grave and climb into it.

What do you want from her? It didn't feel like a simple exchange for the bounty on her head. A thousand dollars might be enough to sway the loyalties of a few two-bit, seat-of-their-pants riders, but this felt more ominous. The truth was, Garth could have snatched Annabelle weeks ago to turn her in for the money. Instead, he'd stuck around, biding his time while he ingratiated himself with the entire crew.

And me. The cowboy's idol worship had been all too convincing. Ethan's heart grew heavy in his chest as he traced the bandit's actions all the way back to his and Annabelle's wedding day.

The "escape" from the stagecoach could have been planned in advance to befriend Annabelle and gain her trust. It certainly would explain how the rogue had avoided taking a single bullet from the gang of bandits pursuing them.

But why had he waited so long to make his move on her? Unless he still wanted something.

The watch! The same watch that had been listed on the Wanted poster. The same watch they'd ransacked his cabin for. The watch Garth Swingler had now kidnapped Annabelle to possess.

Unfortunately for him, the letter had long since been removed, and the railroad spur was in the process of being transferred to her husband's name.

Mine.

Annabelle's father's attorney had been overjoyed to hear of her marriage. He'd assured her via telegram that the paperwork to start the transfer process would be in the mail the next day. It had taken a full month to reach El Vaquero for her signature, and it was currently en route back to the attorney. Within days, Ethan and his bride would be in possession of a dowry that would keep on giving so long as the railroad spur remained profitable.

But both Garth Swingler and the unscrupulous Mr. Featherfall were yet unaware that the game was over. With how long Annabelle had lived in squalor in Atlanta, Mr. Featherfall must have guessed her ignorance concerning the railroad spur. Hence, his pressure for her to wed him. When she'd refused, he'd likely determined that all he truly needed was her father's watch.

He was still looking for the watch, plain and simple, and now Garth Swingler — who was likely in his employ — had his hands on it. Coldness seeped through Ethan's chest. It was only a matter of time before the two criminals discovered that they'd lost. And when they did, heaven only knew what they would do to the innocent woman Garth had kidnapped.

It's happening again. Terror clawed through Ethan, bringing him pain like he'd never felt before. The loss of his first wife had left him reeling, yet he'd managed to get back to some semblance of living. He didn't see that happening again if he failed to get Annabelle back.

All of his hopes and dreams for the future were anchored in her. Funny how it had taken her kidnapping to make him realize this. Without her, the railroad spur would be nothing more than a blasted railroad spur. He needed her to be happy. Her. Just her.

The next thirty minutes or so passed in a flurry of preparations. Ethan galloped back to the ranch to fill the Fords in on what had happened. It came as no surprise when they insisted it wasn't safe for him to go after his wife alone. In the end, Ethan, Jameson, and Keegan saddled up to pursue Annabelle and Garth east. Meanwhile, multiple patrols would remain on vigil, scouring every inch of El Vaquero and the surrounding area.

On their way down the mountain, the three riders passed

by the church where Ethan and Annabelle had exchanged their vows. Bo Stanley came barreling out the front door. His raccoon skin cap was askew, and his bushy reddish brown beard was bristling with energy.

He held up a hand to halt their party. "Lance rode through here a few minutes ago to let me know about Annabelle's capture. I'd like to pray for traveling mercies, if you'll let me."

Ethan's jaw tightened. "Sorry, reverend. There's no time. The man who took her has at least an hour's head start."

Bo stalked forward stubbornly to stand directly in front of his horse. "There's always time to pray, my friend."

"What's the point?" Ethan slapped the air. "I've been to enough funerals. I already know what you're going to say." He snarled out the scripture he was most familiar with from the book of Job. "The Lord giveth and the Lord taketh away. Blessed be the Name of the Lord." He danced Ranger forward a few steps, hoping that Bo would step aside and let them pass.

"Eh, that might very well be the most misquoted scripture in the Bible," Bo scoffed, still not budging. "It wasn't written for funerals. It was a profound statement of a man's faith when his back was against the wall, which I believe yours is."

Thank you for the reminder. A fresh wave of dread swept through Ethan. "What's your point?"

Bo jutted his bushy beard at him. "My point is that Job decided to serve God, no matter what. He chose to put God first, no matter what. And only after He made that decision, did the real miracles begin. The healing of his body. The restoration of his family and wealth. The return of his peace and happiness. There's a powerful lesson in there somewhere, gentlemen." He glanced over at Jameson and Keegan to include them in the statement.

Maybe it was nothing more than Ethan's desperation at work, but Bo's words resonated in his heart. "So, what are you saying, reverend?" His sense of urgency to hit the road was rivaled by the temptation to hear more about the troubling alternative his friend had presented.

"I'm saying you have a choice, Vasquez. You can branch out there into the unknown on your own, not knowing for sure where you're even headed, much less what you're going to find when you get there. Or," he raised a beefy finger to stab the air at Ethan, "you can allow me to lead you in a prayer of faith, where we invite the Keeper of the sun, moon, and stars to accompany you on your search."

Ethan was staggered. As sure as he was sitting there, he'd only made it this far in life by employing his own wits and brawn. But if there was a better way, he owed it to Annabelle to take it.

He gestured hurriedly at Bo. "Go on and pray your blessing over us. What can it hurt?"

"Not a thing. Now get off your horse."

"What?" Ethan glanced anxiously eastward, knowing they needed to be on their way. "I already said there's no time."

"Then make time. The Lord isn't interested in some drive-by, half-baked profession from you. What better way to prove you mean business than by sacrificing a few minutes of the time you could've spent riding toward Annabelle?"

"So help me, Bo!" Ethan was prepared to dig in his heels and run right over the fellow if he didn't hurry up and move out of the way.

Bo held his gaze. "Here's another verse in the Bible. *The Lord will not leave the guilty unpunished. His way is in the whirlwind and the storm, and the clouds are the dust of his feet.* That means He made the world, Ethan. He controls the time, the weather, your life, and mine. You have nothing to lose and everything to gain by getting off your horse."

"Very well." Gritting his teeth, Ethan slid to the ground. "Now what?"

"Kneel with me." Bo nodded at Jameson and Keegan to do the same. "All of you. We need to do this right, for both Annabelle's sake and mine." His lips twitched. "Something tells me I won't have a job much longer if you don't bring her safely home after this stunt."

Ethan closed his eyes, willing the fellow to get on with it. As Bo prayed, however, it was more than just nice words coming out of his mouth. Something happened. Something real.

Peace crept over their small huddle — not just the calmness that comes from the reassurance of well-meaning friends, but something more. For the first time since Annabelle's disappearance, Ethan tasted genuine hope that they were going to find her in time.

"Amen," Bo intoned gruffly.

"Amen," Ethan echoed. It was a foreign word to him, one he'd never uttered before. "What does that word even mean?"

"It means *so be it*. Or, *let it be so*."

"Let it be so," Ethan repeated, feeling a surge of conviction. "We're going to find her, Bo." He was sure of it.

"Yes, but only because you made the right choice today." He stood and waved them back onto their horses. "Go! You're ready now. God be with you, my friends!"

ANNABELLE SPENT THE NEXT SEVERAL HOURS RIDING with a blindfold tied over her eyes. It puzzled her that Garth felt the need to hide their surroundings from her. She already knew who her kidnapper was and where he was taking her. Then again, he was teetering on the edge of madness. There was no telling what he was thinking.

Every so often, he pressed the skin of water back into her

hands. "I want you to be awake for what comes next." Another one of his inane chuckles slid out of him.

"What is coming next?" She doubted he planned to tell her, but she had to ask.

"You'll see," he promised gleefully.

The hoot of a train sounded in the distance.

"Almost there," he crooned in her ear for the umpteenth time.

He slowed his horse to a walk and eventually to a halt. The sound of the train grew closer. It chugged along the tracks, sounding like it was gaining speed.

Garth hopped to the ground and reached up to lift Annabelle down in front of him. "Walk," he commanded, shoving her to get her moving.

Alarm bells sounded inside her head at the realization that he was instructing her to walk toward the approaching train. She took a few stumbling steps, then stopped.

"I said walk!" He raised his voice.

"A train is coming."

"Yes. Isn't it wonderful?"

When she refused to move, he roughly shoved her forward.

"Stop, Garth!" she begged. "What are you doing?"

"We're going to stand on the tracks together."

Horror filled her, making her knees shake. "But we'll die!" The toe of her boot stubbed into the first railroad tie.

"Only if you don't tell me what I want to know." He dragged her, protesting, onto the tracks with him while the train continued to chug closer.

"What do you want to know?" she cried.

"Since you obviously removed whatever your father had stored in his watch, where are the dowry papers for this railroad spur?"

The train tooted another warning of its pending arrival. "With my attorney."

"What's his address?"

She rattled it off, hoping she got it right.

"Good. Then everything is in place. The railroad spur will transfer to me when we are wed."

"I am already wed," she reminded.

"It's a mail-order bride contract," he scoffed. "You have a few weeks left to annul it."

"Only if it wasn't consummated. It's too late, Garth."

"It's never too late. You will claim your marriage wasn't consummated and file for the annulment today."

Fury gripped her at his insolence. "No one will believe me, since I am with child!" The moment the words left her mouth, she realized her mistake. Without the hope of marrying her, there was no telling what Garth might do next.

He fell silent, though he continued to hold her captive on the tracks.

"Please," she begged, tears streaming down her cheeks. "Don't do this!" Visions of Ethan danced before her eyes, along with that of her friends in Atlanta. If Garth refused to show her mercy, she would never see any of them again. Ethan would never know about his child, either. With a moan of misery, she gripped her belly with both hands.

The train chugged close enough to vibrate the tracks, and the conductor laid on his horn.

He sees us. The knowledge brought Annabelle no relief. It was too late for him to stop the train.

Please, Lord. Help me! The train rumbled closer, almost upon them.

Annabelle sprang into action, twisting blindly around and shoving at Garth with all of her might. Then she dove from the tracks. Her hands and knees connected with the ground. A vicious tunnel of wind from the passing train whipped at her hair and cheeks, spraying her with sand and small pebbles. Some of them hit her so hard that they stung.

There was no ensuing shout from Garth to give her any indication if he'd leaped to safety in time. She could hear nothing but the roar of the train engines and the clicking of its wheels along the tracks for several minutes.

Then the world settled back into deathly silence.

I should run. Annabelle clawed at her blindfold, pulling it free at last. That's when the truth slammed into her. She should have already been running.

Garth stood and dusted off his knees from the other side of the tracks. His Stetson was missing, and the whole right side of his face was red with abrasions. "You shouldn't have done that." His voice was cold as he stalked back in her direction. "If you'd just let things be, it would already be over. Now you're going to have to wait for the next train."

Why? Annabelle's legs finally churned into motion. She took off running down the side of the tracks in the direction the train had taken. If she followed it long enough, it would eventually lead to a town. And help.

She only made it a short distance before Garth tackled her. For the second time that day, everything went black.

ETHAN AND HIS FRIENDS STRUCK OUT ON THE OPEN range. A few hours passed before they encountered their first fellow travelers. It was none other than Turner King, the U.S. Marshal.

Ethan's gut tightened with wariness. The encounter didn't feel like a coincidence. Was the man part of the plot to kidnap Annabelle and steal her inheritance?

Mr. King raised a hand in greeting. "I don't reckon you gentlemen know anything about the bandit on a horse who passed by here not too long ago? There have been two different sightings reported."

Ethan's interest piqued. "What did he look like?"

The marshal turned his attention to Ethan. "He had a blindfolded woman on his horse. Does that sound familiar?"

Though Ethan's heart leaped with hope, his blood boiled in his veins at the mention of a blindfold. "His name is Garth Swingler, and the woman he kidnapped is my wife."

"Interesting. Did you marry again since we last spoke, Mr. Vasquez?" The humor in the marshal's voice wasn't reflected in his gaze.

"Begging your pardon, marshal, but I didn't know if you could be trusted the first time we met. I had just been informed that there was a warrant out for my wife's arrest for a crime she didn't commit."

"It has since been revoked, I can assure you."

Relief made Ethan's shoulders sag. "Did you have something to do with that, sir?"

"I am not at liberty to discuss an ongoing investigation, Mr. Vasquez." However, Mr. King's smile held a note of undeniable warmth.

"My wife is the heir to a railroad spur." Ethan watched for the man's reaction.

There was none. He wasn't the least bit surprised. "That is my understanding per her case file."

Case file? Ethan wished the marshal had been more forthcoming about this information weeks ago. Then again, his own antics at the time hadn't given the man much reason to trust him, either. "In her father's will, he decreed that the ownership of the spur would pass to her husband when she wed."

"Making you a very wealthy man, Mr. Vasquez."

"I couldn't care less about a stinking pile of railroad ties, Mr. King. All I want is my wife back." Ethan's voice was raw. "If you know anything about her whereabouts, I am begging you..." His voice broke.

The marshal nodded gravely at him and the Ford brothers. "Follow me, gentlemen."

Exchanging curious looks, Ethan, Jameson, and Keegan dug their heels into their horses' flanks.

They rode for less than a mile before they reached the rest of the men in the marshal's party. All three were bent over a set of train tracks, hacking and sawing at something.

As Ethan rode closer, he could make out the figure of a woman. "Annabelle!" he shouted, leaping from Ranger and breaking into a sprint. "Annabelle!" *Could it be her?*

"Ethan?" The woman on the tracks weakly raised her head. It was her alright. A scratched and bruised version of her with her eyelids swollen from weeping.

"Sweetheart!" Shoving two of the men aside, Ethan crouched down beside her on the tracks. Her hat was missing and her blonde hair was blowing across her face. A pale brown blanket covered her from her chin to her boots.

As he gently tucked her hair back from her face, he heard the marshal order Jameson and Keegan to continue riding down the tracks in the effort to stop the next train.

Right. Ethan's heart shuddered in his chest. There was always another train on its way. It could be days, hours, or even minutes.

As he examined the condition his wife was in, it occurred to him that minutes might not be enough. It wasn't a pale brown blanket covering her, as he originally thought. It was an unbroken line of ropes. They were binding every inch of her limbs and torso. That's what the marshal's men were hacking and sawing at.

Ethan reached for the blade he kept tucked inside one of his boots and joined their efforts. So did the marshal. As they put their backs into it, Annabelle explained in a tremulous voice how she came to be in her current predicament.

"I should have pretended to go along with his madness," she concluded wearily.

"I'm not sure it would've made any difference, darlin'. He's a monster, one who deserves to swing from a rope."

"To be honest, I felt a little sorry for him," she sighed. "Despite everything he did to me, I think the real monster is still back in Atlanta. Mr. Featherfall set his own son up to take the fall for his crimes. It's no wonder Garth is so twisted up in the head."

Ethan was awash with admiration over her endless capacity for kindness. "The pureness of your heart is one of the reasons I love you so much, Annabelle."

"You do?" Her blue gaze brightened with hope. "I wasn't sure if such a thing was possible."

He shot her an incredulous look. "It would be impossible *not* to love you, darlin'!"

"I was a mail-order bride," she reminded. "You never laid eyes on me before we met at the altar."

"I remember that day well. Believe me, my heart never stood a chance against your loveliness." Her tearful smile made him saw all the harder at the rope he was working on, making it pop loose. Then he set his blade to the next one and began again.

Despite his efforts and that of the marshal and his men, it was slow progress cutting through so many ropes. They were some of the thickest ropes Ethan had ever encountered. It took a good twenty minutes or so just to free his wife on one side. Though it made it easier for her to breathe, one arm and one leg remained firmly bound to the railroad ties.

Then the unthinkable happened. The hoot of an

approaching train sounded — faint at first, but it grew louder. Annabelle paled and caught her lower lip between her teeth. She rolled to her side, tugging furiously at the ropes.

"Hold still, darlin'." Ethan sawed as fast as he could. "Jameson and Keegan rode up the tracks. They'll stop the train in time. You'll see."

The train hooted again.

"And if they don't succeed?" Her voice shook.

"They will." All five men hacked and sawed with every ounce of strength in them as the train grew closer.

Annabelle's expression went blank, and she sagged back to the tracks. "You need to go. All of you. Save yourselves."

None of them stopped sawing.

"I mean it." Her voice took on a deathly calm note. "I appreciate all you've done. I do. But you are somebody's husbands, fathers, or sons. You are still needed. Not all of us have to perish here today."

"I'm not leaving you." Ethan swung his blade, slashing at the ropes with renewed fury. Two more of them snapped off.

"Please, Ethan. I want you to live." A sheen of dampness covered the deep blue of her gaze. "I've never in my life been happier than I was while living in your cabin on your beautiful mountain. It was worth it. Even if I knew it would end like this, I would sign that infernal mail-order bride contract and do it all over again."

Tears burned behind his eyelids at her words. "It's not going to end here, sweetheart. I won't let it." He started hacking so wildly with his knife that one of the men scooted back with an expulsion of alarm.

"Go," she urged the marshal and his men again. "I want you to live. I want all of you to live."

As the train rolled closer, Ethan could hear Jameson and Keegan shouting at the top of their lungs. A quick glance their way proved they were riding on opposite sides of the tracks, waving their shirts and bellowing for the train to halt.

From the heavy screeching of wheels against metal, it seemed to Ethan that the conductor was applying his brakes, but there was no way to determine if he would be able to stop before reaching Annabelle.

"Go!" she pleaded again. "There's nothing more you can do for me. If the Lord wills it, the train will stop. If not, I know where I'm heading." Tears rolled down her cheeks and dripped to the ground. "I'll be reunited with my family first and, in time, with you."

Ethan continued to hack at the ropes, even as the other men scooted back. The marshal lingered the longest.

"Go," Ethan growled at him. "She's right. Not all of us need to perish here today." He fully intended to, though, if that's what it boiled down to.

Once the marshal straightened, Ethan had the room to swing his arm and slash all the harder, snapping three more of the ropes.

"Is there nothing I can say to make you leave me?" his wife begged.

"No. I am yours, and you are mine." He positioned himself between her and the oncoming train, not wanting her to look.

She sighed, reaching out to touch his knees that were grinding into the gravel. "Then my only regret is that you'll never get to meet our baby this side of eternity."

His sawing momentarily faltered. "You're in the family way?" he rasped.

She nodded tearfully. "Yes. I wanted to be sure before I told you. Then all of this happened, and I never got the chance—"

A violent burst of strength shot through Ethan from his hat to his boots. Roaring like a lion, he sawed through the final ropes with a single sweep of his arm. Reaching for his wife, he snatched her up from the tracks, rolling with her to safety.

The train screamed past, still struggling to stop. Keegan yanked the reins of his horse and nudged the creature around the spot where Ethan and Annabelle lay, panting and clinging to each other in a patch of prairie grass.

Chapter 10: The Letter

ETHAN

Two new arrest warrants were issued bearing Dale Allard Featherfall and Garth Swingler's names. With U.S. Marshal Turner King on the case, Ethan was confident that the father and son criminal ring would soon be brought to justice.

In the meantime, he and the Fords kept their heightened patrols in place. Additionally, they went to work repairing the damaged windows and doors in his cabin. They extended the back porch to add another pair of rooms while they were at it. One would serve as a nursery and the other as a library and music room. Because of the bookshelves lining three walls, it took the better part of a month to complete the entire project around their regular responsibilities. By then, the rest of the repairs were also completed, and Ethan and Annabelle were able to move back home.

"Why do you keep calling this a music room?" she pressed on their first morning back in the cabin.

It was Saturday. In an unusual turn of events, he'd taken the day off, something he intended to do more often now that he was about to become a father. Annabelle needed him around more. So would their son or daughter.

"I have my reason." He tugged her to the middle of the room in question, reveling in the fact that they were alone at last. Without six extra brothers around to crack jokes every time he touched his bride, he was making up for lost time. He brushed his lips against her eyelids, nose, and cheeks. Then he swooped in to claim her mouth for the tenderest of kisses. But he didn't stop there. He kissed his way down her chin and the side of her neck. Then he slowly nipped his way down both of her arms as he took a knee in front of her. Lacing their fingers together, he pressed their joined hands to her belly.

It was just starting to blossom into roundness. She was wearing a new dress that she and Paloma had sewn for her condition. It could be expanded as needed by loosening a set of satin ribbons they'd threaded through the high-waisted skirts. Ethan loved the dress, not only because his pregnant wife was wearing it, but also because it was his favorite color on her — pink. With her hair pulled up, and only a few curls dangling down, she looked very much the part of the sassy southern belle he'd married.

"My family," he crooned, leaning forward to kiss the spot between where their hands rested.

Annabelle slid her fingers from his to thread them through his hair. "I love you so much, Ethan," she sighed. "I love it here on your mountain. I love our cabin. I love our life together."

"I love it, too. All of it." He kissed her belly again. "You are more than I deserve."

"No, I'm not." She sounded so indignant that he chuckled. "You're a good man, Ethan Vasquez. I am so fortunate that I ended up at the altar with you. I cannot tell you how many times during my journey west that I feared I was making the worst decision of my life."

He smiled. "And then I showed up looking more beast than man, making you question your decision even more." He walked his fingers up her belly. "Couldn't even get a proper kiss out of you on my first try."

"Proper!" she exclaimed, sounding indignant. "Your appearance was downright barbaric. It took a lion's share of fortitude on my part to offer you my cheek. A *proper* southern miss wouldn't have allowed a savage like you to kiss her at all."

"A savage, eh?" He stood, tugging her close again. "I can show you what savage is, madam." He leaned in for a very enthusiastic, very thorough kiss that dragged a breathy sound from her. His heart sang at the sound.

"Very savage," she repeated, giving the hair behind his neck a playful tweak. "Not that I'm complaining." She caught her lower lip between her teeth. "Your savagery is what put a precious babe in my belly."

Before he could come up with a worthy comeback, the sound of a wagon rumbled their way. *Just in time.* He'd left a window in the music room cracked open a few inches so he could listen for the arrival of his very special delivery.

Surprise stained his wife's fine-boned features as she leaned back in his arms to crane at the window. "Are we expecting company?"

"In a manner of speaking, darlin'." It was a set of delivery men, bearing her gift.

Reaching for her hand, he walked with her to the living room and opened the front door. A wagon was resting in front of their cabin, no more than three or four strides from the porch steps.

The driver tipped his hat at them, hollering, "Is this the Vasquez residence?"

"It sure is." Ethan glanced down at his wife to see her reaction to the goings-on in front of them. Her forehead was wrinkled in puzzlement. "I'm glad you made it safely up the mountain." He hoped what he'd ordered had also arrived safely.

"Nice view," the man mused, glancing over the rim of their property at the mountains below.

"Thank you!" Ethan leaned over to mutter in his wife's ear. "I could gaze at my current view all day long, darlin'."

She blushed and lightly swatted his chest. "Behave yourself," she hissed. "We have an audience." Her scolding was swallowed up by a gasp of awe as four sturdy men lifted a pianoforte from the back of their delivery wagon.

"Oh, Ethan!" she squealed, clapping a hand over her mouth. "You didn't!"

He nuzzled the hair behind her ear. "You asked why I kept calling our new room in the back a music room, and I told you I had my reason. Well, this is it."

His heart clenched to see happy tears gather in her eyes. For the next half hour or so, she fluttered like a butterfly around the workmen, instructing them where to place the lovely instrument. Then she hovered while they finished assembling and tuning it.

"Oh, Ethan!" she sighed for the dozenth time when they placed an upholstered bench behind the keys and stepped back.

"You're all set, ma'am." One of the workmen ushered her gallantly toward it.

Ethan grinned at her. "How about you give it a jingle for us, darlin'?"

With a rapturous expression, she gingerly took a seat on the bench and scooted it forward. "Oh, my!" she sighed, running her fingers lovingly over the keys without pushing them down yet. "It's been so long since I got to do this."

Then she pressed down with both hands, and the strains of a familiar melody resounded across the room. Ethan folded his arms and rocked back on his heels, utterly transfixed by how skillfully his wife could play. Her slender fingers roved with confidence over the keys.

When she parted her rosy lips and started to sing straight to him, he thought his heart might burst. She'd filled his life with love and joy, and now she was drenching it with music. He recognized the hymn as one they'd recently sung at Bo's church.

> All things bright and beautiful,
> All creatures great and small,
> All things wise and wonderful,
> The Lord God made them all.

He caressed his wife with his eyes. *I'm so glad He made you, darlin'. You are perfect for me.* Her voice filled the room, surrounding him and making him glad to be alive.

> Each little flower that opens,
> Each little bird that sings,
> He made the glowing colors,
> He made their tiny wings.

She sang the chorus again. Then she played for a moment without singing before launching into another verse. She caught Ethan's eye and smiled. He soon realized why.

> The purple-headed mountain,
> The river running by,
> The sunset and the morning,
> That brightens up the sky.

She was singing out her thanksgiving for the very mountain they lived on. Then she sang the chorus again.

> All things bright and beautiful,
> All creatures great and small,

> All things wise and wonderful,
> The Lord God made them all.

She allowed the final notes to hang in the air. Ethan's heart was overflowing by the time they faded.

The workmen clapped and cheered. One of them looked like he was about to beg for another song, but the oldest member of their crew gave him a warning look. "Can't you tell they're newlyweds? It's time for us to mosey on back to the warehouse."

Annabelle thanked them with fresh-baked biscuits and a jar of plum jam. After the door shut behind the last workman, she spun around to Ethan, her skirts swirling around her blooming figure.

"Oh, Ethan! Thank you! Thank you! Thank you!" She launched herself into his arms.

He caught her against his chest and spun her in a full circle before returning her to her feet. "I didn't know you could sing and play like that." He was in awe of her talent. The mere thought of having such an accomplished woman rearing his children was enough to take his breath away.

She made a face at him. "It's not as practical as milking a cow, mind you."

"Says who?" He grinned at her. "I wouldn't be surprised if our cow doubles her production now that she has such lovely music to listen to."

Minutes later, Lance Ford knocked on the door to deliver the mail he'd fetched from El Gato. "You have a letter, ma'am." He treated Annabelle to a mocking bow. "You may thank me with cookies or bread. Or anything else edible. I'm not overly picky."

She rolled her eyes as she eagerly accepted the letter. "You never fill up, do you?"

His expression turned teasing. "You could sit me down in your kitchen and try, ma'am."

ETHAN TOSSED A PITHY REPLY IN HIS DIRECTION that Annabelle didn't quite catch. Their voices faded as the two of them laughed and wrestled their way into the kitchen.

Appreciating the fact that Ethan understood she needed to be alone for a moment, she tore open the letter and sank onto the sofa to read it. Thanks to a bolt of navy brocade that Paloma had claimed she no longer needed, the sofa had been freshly upholstered. It now looked as fine as the furniture Annabelle had grown up with at her family's plantation in Georgia.

She caught her breath as she read the greeting and opening lines. It sounded like all five of her friends had contributed to the letter. She could almost hear their voices as she read.

Our dearest Annabelle,

We are thrilled to hear you are safe from a certain horrendous creature whose name shall not be named in our letter. We miss you more than you will ever know and cannot wait to see you again, which might be sooner than any of us anticipated.

Poor, poor Penelope finds herself in a dire situation that we fear can only be remedied by her immediate departure from Atlanta. By the time you receive this letter, it is very likely she will have already met with The Western Moon Agency and signed a mail-order bride contract. We are unsure what her chances are of being sent to the same town as you, but we are hoping and praying for such a miracle. Wouldn't it be utterly delightful to have us all together again?

Nibbling her lower lip with worry, Annabelle read their description of Penelope's dilemma. Apparently, a ring of pickpockets were claiming she was encroaching on their territory due to a number of robberies she'd prevented in the park across the street from the boarding house. They were now following, harassing, and threatening her to pay them back for the "income" she'd cost them.

Annabelle dropped the letter in her lap, her mind racing over the possibilities. It's where Ethan found her after finally herding Lance out the front door.

"What's wrong, darlin'?" He took a knee in front of her and reached for her hand.

"I have reason to believe that my friend Penelope is in as much trouble as I was before leaving Atlanta, maybe more." Annabelle pressed a hand to her rapidly beating heart. "I'm terribly worried about her."

Ethan cradled her hand between his. "I might be a lowly range rider, but I have ears to listen if you care to tell me about it."

Annabelle gulped. "She's gone and signed a mail-order bride contract with the same agency I did. I don't know what her chances are of wedding a man in El Vaquero, but nothing would make me happier."

Ethan studied her, frowning. "I might be able to increase her chances."

Annabelle's eyes widened. "How so?"

"Do you remember how Jameson introduced me to the attorney working in proxy for The Western Moon Agency in El Gato? I see no reason why we can't pay the man a visit and pass on your request."

"Oh, yes, please!" Annabelle clapped her hands excitedly. "The very thought of having Penelope here when the baby comes is, well, almost too good to be true."

Ethan pushed off the floor to take a seat beside her on the

sofa. "I, too, would appreciate you having an extra set of hands around when the baby comes."

Annabelle tipped her head adoringly against his shoulder. "I reckon all that's left for us to do is find her the perfect husband here in El Vaquero."

He cuddled her close. "Isn't that the agency's job?"

"Yes, but there's no reason we can't do a little advertising of our own."

"Advertising?" Her husband arched one dark eyebrow at her.

"Penelope looks like a fairy princess, Ethan! Plus, she's so witty she can make your sides hurt from laughing. If it wasn't for the war, she would've long since been married and—"

He pressed a finger to her lips to halt her tirade. "If I repeat what you just told me, there will be a mile-long stampede of cowboys throwing their hat in the ring for her hand in marriage. Are you sure that's what you want?"

"Yes, indeed! Then she can have her pick of the litter, so to speak."

ETHAN WASN'T ENTIRELY SURE PENELOPE WOULD BE doing the picking, though he didn't want to say anything to dim his wife's hopes in that direction. He'd stumbled across a very interesting piece of information during his visit to the attorney working in proxy for The Western Moon Agency — the agency owner's name, of all things. He'd caught a brief glimpse of it when the attorney had opened and closed an important looking folder.

He swallowed a chuckle. *If the agency owner is who I think she is, she'll marry your friend to a Ford brother, or my name isn't Ethan Vasquez.*

But that was a mystery he could continue to puzzle

through in the coming days. Right now, he had his wife all to himself, and he planned to take full advantage of that fact.

He stood and reached for Annabelle's hand to pull her to her feet. He towed her to the center of the room.

"What are you doing?" Her blue gaze was utterly mystified.

He leaned closer to croon in her ear, "May I have this dance, Mrs. Vasquez?"

A breathy chuckle escaped her. "But we don't have any music."

"Then you can sing to me."

"I am fairly certain you don't know how to dance, either."

"Teach me, darlin'." He spun her in a slow circle to get them started.

She faced him and placed one hand on his shoulder and the other hand in his hand. It didn't take him long to catch the rhythm and learn the first few steps she demonstrated. It was as if they'd been made to dance together.

After a short lesson full of more laughter and kisses than any actual instruction, Ethan sashayed with her toward the window, so they could gaze at the mountains together. The sun was pouring across the peaks, making them glow like gold.

Even so, their beauty in no way compared to the breathtaking woman in his arms. He breathed a silent prayer of thanksgiving that Bo Stanley had set him straight on a few important matters recently.

I am hers, she is mine, and we are yours, Lord. Forever and ever. Amen.

Thank you for reading
Cowboy for Annabelle.

A mail-order bride decides her best protection from a dangerous enemy is to win the heart of her mail-order groom in ***Cowboy for Penelope.***

Sneak Preview: Cowboy for Penelope

MAIL ORDER BRIDES ON THE RUN #2

August, 1867

The name of the man I'm about to marry sounds...interesting.
Dignified.
Serious.
Kindhearted, if she was fortunate.

Penelope stifled a shiver of apprehension as she unfolded the mail-order bride contract in her lap again. It was growing wrinkled from the number of times she'd read it already, but she couldn't help taking another peek — especially since she'd be meeting the gentleman in question at the altar today.

Today!

She tried to swallow the tightness in her throat, wishing she knew what he looked like or what his voice sounded like. However, the contract didn't give her so much as a hint about such things. At the moment, it was entirely up to her imagination to fill in the details as she traced a finger over the words in the legal agreement she was holding.

I, Penelope Copeland, agree to wed Jameson Ford of Ford Ranch in El Vaquero, Texas. Farmer and rancher. Age 27.

The starchy secretary at the mail-order bride agency in Atlanta had said he and his five brothers made their living from rounding up the wild longhorn cattle in the area. She hadn't made it sound like the Fords were wealthy — not if they were scavenging the countryside for every last creature they added to their herd.

Penelope blew out a silent sigh, trying to take comfort in the fact that the Fords were landowners, at least. Granted, it was the dry, rocky land of the wild west, probably chock full of rattlesnakes. Even so, they were better off than she was.

Or so she hoped.

The only reason she'd agreed to marry a rugged cowboy, sight unseen, was because the agency had granted her one request — to be matched with a man who lived and worked in El Vaquero. It was the same town her best friend, Annabelle, had been sent a few months earlier as a mail-order bride.

Penelope had every intention of seeing for herself that her friend was being treated well by her new husband. If she wasn't, well, that was the sole reason Penelope was traveling with no less than two pistols in her reticule. Despite all the manners that had been drummed into the heads of southern girls since birth, they were far from the helpless creatures many folks assumed them to be.

Taking comfort in that thought, she smoothed a hand down the rumpled skirt of her favorite olive green gown, longing for an iron to set it to rights. Once upon a time, she'd performed a charade in this very dress — with a gallant young bachelor, no less, that everyone had expected her to marry someday. That was before the war had bankrupted her family, of course, turning her into a social outcast.

Though the green gown served as a depressing reminder of

days gone by, she still adored the medieval cut of its sleeves and the lovely gold buttons running from her elbows to her wrists. Maybe it was foolish of her to wear it to her wedding, considering another man had once courted her in it. However, it was her finest dress. She had no better options.

The last she'd heard, Mr. Dalton Fancy Pants Gentry was courting some sinfully plain, albeit disgustingly rich, oldest daughter of a shipping tycoon. Apparently, the war had taken a toll on his family's bank accounts, as well. She was hard put to sympathize with his plight, however. While she and her closest friends had been orphaned and reduced to working-class girls, he was still dancing his nights away in the Gentry plantation's second-story ballroom. Or so she'd heard.

In recent months, it had become increasingly difficult to keep up with the latest gossip about the social whirl in Atlanta. She'd been too busy making a living with her washboard.

She tucked the mail-order bride contract back in her pocket and splayed her fingers out in front of her. *Mercy!* There was a blister on the side of her right thumb that was trying its hardest to turn into a callus. She'd spent the entire week and a half on the train trying to coax the skin back to buttery softness with a bottle of lotion her friend, Eliza Jane, had unearthed as a farewell gift.

The train wheels rumbled beneath her seat, rolling her ever closer to El Gato, Texas — the closest train depot to the mountain town where her future husband lived. With each passing mile, her apprehension grew, and her silent prayers became more desperate.

Please, God, let my new husband be a kind man. And if it's not too much trouble, let him have a sense of humor. In the next moment, it dawned on her that it might be too late to pray for such things, considering that the deed was done. Her husband had already been picked, and he'd already footed the bill for her train fare and modest travel allowance. Even so, she could hardly stand the thought of being tied for the rest of her days to some poker-faced crabapple.

About that sense of humor, God...

A commotion at the far end of the car yanked her thoughts away from her fretting and back to the present. A boy yelled, a man shouted back, and the sounds of a wrestling match ensued. Like the other passengers, she swung around to determine what was amiss.

It was impossible to see more than the heads and shoulders of the passengers standing between the scufflers and her bench at the front of the car.

"What's going on?" she murmured, utterly mystified as she balanced on her knees in the seat with her elbows propped on the top of the cushion. Not only was it an unladylike pose, it proved to be a fruitless gesture. She still couldn't see anything beyond the broad shoulders of her mostly male fellow passengers.

The grandfatherly fellow who'd been sitting across from her the entire trip made a harrumphing sound. "Probably another stowaway." His mouth beneath his silver handlebar mustache turned down in disapproval.

"A stowaway!" Sensing a story, Penelope hastily whirled around to reclaim her seat, smoothing her skirts around her ankles once again. "You don't sound surprised."

"I'm not." He shrugged, making the threadbare fabric of his suit jacket rise and fall over his faded blue shirt. "With how many street rats are scurrying around Atlanta these days, it's inevitable that a few of the little varmints found their way on board."

"Street rats, you say?" Penelope's heart thumped with foreboding. She hoped it was simply a poor choice of words on his part. To her, the term *street rat* was synonymous with *pickpocket*.

"Thieves!" His distaste was nearly palatable. "Why, just the other day, they clobbered a man within an inch of his life for his pocket watch." Her fellow traveler shook his head sadly. "It was a family heirloom, and he'll probably never see it again."

Penelope's heart raced sickly at the clarification that he was, indeed, referring to the homeless, dangerous creatures who roamed the city streets all hours of the day and night — stealing instead of working honest jobs — a choice of vocations that paid far better than the laundry and mending she and her friends took in.

A lot better.

Which was how she'd ended up in the pickle that had ultimately compelled her to sign a mail-order bride contract. According to the gang of pickpockets who worked in the park across the street from her boarding house, the number of thefts she'd prevented in recent months had cut heavily into their profiteering. So much so that they'd threatened to do her bodily harm if she didn't stop warning folks to hold on tighter to their valuables when they passed through the park.

Swallowing hard, she craned her neck to peer over the seat again. "What will happen to the stowaways?"

"No telling." The older gentleman waved his hands in disgust. "If it were up to me, I'd turn them over to the sheriff in El Gato. More'n likely, though, they'll end up back on the street."

"Here in Texas?" Penelope swallowed a gasp, hoping she'd heard wrong.

"Unfortunately, Miss."

"Pickpockets from Atlanta," she repeated carefully, "could end up on the streets of El Gato, you say?" Oh, this was bad! Very, very bad!

"Or El Vaquero. Or any of the other surrounding communities." The older gentleman gave the end of his mustache a thoughtful twirl.

El Vaquero? A wave of lightheadedness shook her. *Surely not!* She couldn't imagine a pair of street urchins, who depended on stolen goods as their main source of income, heading for a remote mountain town like El Vaquero. It made more sense for them to continue menacing the streets of bigger, more populated areas, didn't it?

She sank into her seat once again, no longer worried about what her future husband looked like or if he was kind, funny, good looking, or hopelessly bald and toothless. If the stowaways on the train were pickpockets, she had far bigger problems to worry about.

Start reading
Cowboy for Penelope
today!

About Jovie

Jovie Grace is an Amazon bestselling author of sweet and inspirational historical romance books full of faith, hope, and cowboys. She also writes sweet contemporary romance as Jo Grafford.

For the most up-to-date printable list of her sweet historical books:
Click here
or go to:
https://www.jografford.com/joviegracebooks

For the most up-to-date printable list of her sweet contemporary books:
Click here
or go to:
https://www.JoGrafford.com/books

Happy reading!

- amazon.com/stores/Jovie-Grace/author/B09SB1V58Q
- bookbub.com/authors/jovie-grace
- facebook.com/JovieGraceBooks

Made in the USA
Monee, IL
17 September 2025